I0579520

RADAR ROAD:

The Best of *On Impulse*

Short Stories

By NATH JONES

Edited and Arranged by
MORGAN SORVILLO KIGER

LIFE LIST PRESS

CHICAGO · 2016

Life List Press
Chicago, IL

PREVIOUSLY PUBLISHED

Jones, Nath. "Norma L." *From the Edge of the
Prairie* 4 (2007): 69-76. Print.

PUBLISHER'S NOTE
These selections are works of fiction. Names,
characters, places, and incidents are either the
product of the author's imagination or are used
fictionally and any resemblance to actual persons,
living or dead, business establishments, events, or
locales is entirely coincidental

ISBN-13: 978-1-937316-10-5

Book design by Gin Y. Havard
Author photo by Louisa Podlich
Cover image by Yulia Drozdova

PUBLISHED IN THE UNITED STATES OF
AMERICA

For Our Loved Ones

(you know who you are)

TABLE OF CONTENTS

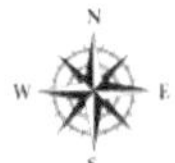

There is a time before the choices are
made when we can all be friends.

ORDERLY

Here I am at the end of a wonderful life. And this is the way I want things. I still look pretty good for my age. Must have been all the years of laughing with my husband. He is doddering around here somewhere and I am enjoying a few minutes of sunlight on the back porch. There is a warbler in the cherry tree and I can almost see all the springs with their warblers passing through.

My husband has just come into the room but seems to have forgotten something and is leaving again. I am smiling at his frail intensity and remembering all the years we've shared as the sun filters onto the lawn.

He's back now. Satisfied by whatever accomplishment he made. There is no evidence of whatever it was, but he kisses me on the top of my head and pats my shoulder with an arthritic hand. And as if any activity might be superior to stillness he moves around behind me and draws the blinds so that the sunlight is no longer with us, blinding.

I would rather have enjoyed the sun—its warmth and emboldened light—for another hour. But it is no matter. He leans on my shoulder and strains to turn on a lamp next to me. It is what he wants me to want. It is the way I will likely want things in an hour when the warmth and boldness of my golden lawn have disappeared into the blue-gray garage shadow.

My husband does not notice sunsets. He cares about what time it is and tends to my evening, as is his habit. He is concentrating and too distracted to take my hand as he offers me nothing in particular but assures that my book, my newspaper, my basket of knitting, the remote for the television, a card from our granddaughter, and my teacup are all within easy reach. They are all here, all the choices I could ever call out for him to come and find.

I stare at the drawn blind, hating the lamplight.

Satisfied with my well-being, he trots off again to busy himself in another room.

NORMA L.

The farm road ended somewhere not too pretty but sometimes lit well by the rising and setting of the sun. Before its end, the road branched off from old asphalt becoming oiled limestone, loosening, rising over railroad tracks, winding around property lines, and finally branching again muddy and mossy, spreading out in the shadow of a brick-faced duplex, where instead of existing side-by-side, one apartment perched on top of another. Parked there next to each other under a few isolated oak trees on the final damp pitch were two cars: a black Corvette and a light blue Buick. The Corvette was covered in three years of oak bits and dust motes. The Buick was just washed yesterday.

Under a yellow bulb every night, a door lit by reflected moth wings led into the lower apartment. On the side of the building, in shadow, an old handmade set of wooden stairs went up to Norma L.'s apartment.

Norma was sixty-two. She sat at her dinner table prepared for a wedding anniversary, staring at a candlestick. It was vibrating. She tried to ignore it.

The phone rang and in one of thirty-eight years' worth of subsequent evening phone calls someone more than familiar said, "Almost home, sweetie. Had a spill right as I was leaving."

So she waited, ignoring the vibrations of the candlestick, ignoring irritation at the effect on a pleasant summer evening, ignoring magazine covers and headlines about kids, just kids— ignoring it all.

Instead she turned her mind backwards to an old white dress still hanging in a closet, to a

pair of real silk pantyhose two sizes too small.
Back to nervous, unwrinkled hands holding on to
each other at an altar. Her fingers moved out to
the base of the candlestick and felt it
unconsciously. She opened the years like a nesting
doll and assembled them again in her mind.

She tried to remember pleasant things
seen and done, but the vibrations kept her in the
present. She tried to concentrate lovingly on her
favorite great-aunt who had given the candlesticks
as a wedding present. But she could not. The
chair vibrated. And her elbows vibrated where she
leaned them on the table. And her chin vibrated
where she leaned her chin on her hands.

Standing in the open door, having
overcome the stairs, her husband said, "He's at it
again, huh?"

"Yep. About two hours."

Mr. L. shut the door and fixed the kind of
little rug which is so often defeated by the
opening of doors. "There was a spill, which would
have been my excuse to make it to the florist and
get here just a few minutes late. But then there

really was a spill, and so I had to clean the mess up, and then head over to the florist. Of course, they had just closed so I had to go around back and pound on the loading dock door until they let me in. I would have gotten the flowers at lunch but they wouldn't have been so fresh then, which Frank understood. And he already had them ready for me anyway, and I had cash. But all told, it made me more than late. So. I'm sorry." This was all explained to the floor and the arrangement of the little rug. Turning to his wife Mr. L. said, "Happy anniversary." He tried not to yawn as he handed his wife the white and pink bouquet.

Moving across the old linoleum, he forgot to kiss her and was already lifting pot lids and snooping in the oven. "This smells great."

Mr. L. stood stoic but vibrating in the middle of the room. He looked at his wife. "I could go down and say something to him. I could be nice. I could ask for an hour on account of our anniversary."

"Don't you dare. You've got no right. He pays his rent, and you're not his daddy."

"Fine. 'Cause those stairs nearly killed me the first time. My knees are— What we should have done was rent the top out too and just moved into town."

"Affects the taxes."

"Those stairs are taxing me half to death. It was one thing with us on the bottom and the kid up here. But between his god-awful ugly choice of furniture and those stairs, I just don't know how long this arrangement'll hold up. And what are we gonna do when they freeze? You want a new hip for Christmas?"

"Those stairs are doing you a service. You've lost at least five pounds. It's good for you. Good for your heart."

"It's good for my memory too. 'Cause I'll tell you. I don't forget anything in the truck anymore. I sit there and think and decide what needs to go up, and I take it all, and if I do end up forgetting something I just leave it."

"Quit bitching so much. Just be glad you can get up those stairs, you old crank. I've made

you a nice dinner, now, and the least you can do is
sit down and enjoy it."

"I know you've been waiting. But I just
have to take a shower or I won't feel at all right.
Will she keep another twenty minutes?"

She nodded.

She vibrated as she leaned against the
sink. She opened the green tissue paper and cut
the rubber band. Free, the greenery rolled over
itself on the drain board. Tulips thick-folded in
their own leaves tried not to bloom just yet.
Lanky rose stems seemed unnatural stripped of
their thorns. She cut the stems of the bouquet to
fit her favorite vase and broken pieces of lily of
the valley instilled a little relief. Norma's feet
vibrated from the kid's music. She sighed and
hesitated with scissors opened around a thick
stem, water running. Her eyes filled with tears,
and she cut the stem as quickly as she could. She
left the rest of the stems alone and so the bouquet
was like a stair step, half the right height and half
too tall.

Giving up arranging, Mrs. L. sat down and stared at the television. The couch vibrated. The coffee table vibrated. The television vibrated. Mr. L. came out from the tiny bathroom dressed nicely and stood near the television combing his hair. He pulled his shirt out and re-tucked it, loosening the belt one notch. He was vibrating.

"What's for dinner?"

"Pot roast."

Mrs. L. lit the candles and flipped off the overhead light.

Mr. L. pulled out the chair for his wife. She sat down and put a napkin in her lap. Mr. L. patted both her shoulders with both his hands and kissed the top of her head. "It smells good."

He stood behind her and yawned.

He sat down next to her and looked at the flowers. "Seems like Frank does a nice job, but I guess I should have got there before the shop closed. These look all cockeyed somehow. Sorry."

She laughed. "No. Frank did not sell you cockeyed flowers. I just only cut half the stems to fit the vase."

"Why not cut them all?"

"I don't know. I guess I just couldn't."

Mr. L. suppressed another yawn.

The candlesticks vibrated on the table. Light danced on the ceiling. They sat without serving each other.

Norma said, "Remember Aunt Ginny?"

Mr. L. scratched his bald spot. "She was something. Good Christian."

"Nobody ever knew it."

"Best kind."

She laughed again. "So you thought Frank sold you some bum flowers for my anniversary, huh? He wouldn't dare. He knows better. His arrangement was prettier than mine. But just a bit too tall. I was trying to cut it down is all. If he sold you bum anniversary flowers, he'd be out of business quick. Anniversary flowers is about all he does sell. And funeral flowers, I guess. But we don't need to start saving money for those, thank the Lord. Not just yet."

Somehow they sat on their years together, each one staring at the nearest vibrating candlestick.

"Some things just can't be helped. The spill held me up."

"You tired?"

"A bit. Might just be the heat. Shower helped."

The windows vibrated.

"We've been through more than our share together, wouldn't you say, Mom?"

"More than a bit. More than our share."

The ceramic salt and pepper shakers on the back of the stove vibrated.

"Mom," Mr. L was cautious. "I could ask him for an hour. I really don't mind to. It's your anniversary. You deserve to have some peace in your own home."

"And he doesn't?" The moths by the downstairs door swirled around the aluminum-shaded bulb. Aspirants of their kind bumped against the upstairs windows. "He's just a kid."

"I know it. But I'm just an old man. And you're just an old woman."

"I'm not just anything."

They laughed.

She picked up his plate to begin serving. They looked at each other and vibrated. She put the plate back down and stood up. Her husband took her by the hand, walked her to the door, and they made their way slowly one in front of the other down the outside stairs. They stood at the bottom of the stairs looking at the oak trunks in the last bit of daylight.

"Thanks for washing my car."

"It wasn't quite warm enough for the wax. But it looks pretty good between his sorry old Vette and my sorry old truck."

"The Vette's not old at all."

"Well, it's looked a hell of a lot better than it does now."

"Maybe you could wash it for him. Take it and get it cleaned up a bit."

"Not until he asks me to. And even then it might not run."

"It'll run." The bark on the trunks began to fade. The details loosened their grip. "He did drive crazy, didn't he?"

"What a fool he was. Remember when he drove it right through the rusted cemetery fence? Has that been five years?"

They laughed hard. Mr. L. retold her the familiar story at the edge of the moth light. "He came running up the lane shouting, banging on the door. 'Mr. L., get the winch. Get the winch and bring the dually!'"

They laughed remembering the night. Mr. L. went on. "He was scared shitless. Hadn't had a thing to drink. Not a thing. Just took that gravel corner too quick, and don't you know he cleared the ditch completely, he told me, and ran his damned Vette all into that old pack of graves."

Country graveyards nestle themselves here and there between corn and Queen Anne's lace in places like this. Mr. L. had joyful tears in his eyes recalling again. "I got the winch and the dually and you were out there in your rollers with the deer light. Remember?"

She was giggling and nodding.

He went on. "I'll never forget his face. Not contorted really. Not worried looking. Not about to admit how scared he was. Just jaw clenched and eyes blown wide open like a damned squirrel treed by a Siberian Laika. He loved that car. Spent a half-hour trying to figure how he was gonna get that big old chain wrapped around the front bumper without messing up her paint job. Stuffing chamois cloths everywhere. Shaking so hard. I had to do it for him. Remember? Oh Lord. What a night. And remember after all that, the three of us looking at those gravestones after we finally got the car out on the road? Remember?"

Norma L., laughing hard with her hand over her mouth, took over the story, "Oh, don't I ever. We were so concerned getting the car out I don't think it crossed any of our minds about those headstones. But his face when he realized it. I don't think I've ever laughed so hard. Not ever."

They laughed remembering. The oaks stepped back into the night.

Mr. L. reclaimed the story. "And remember how he just started pulling up those damned stones trying to put them to rights?"

"Wouldn't have mattered. That marble with the burnt-rubber tire tracks on it would have stood out more standing up than laying down anyway."

"But he did try his damnedest, didn't he?"

"He's a good kid."

"I know."

"Remember him that next week?"

Norma L. leaned against the house from laughing so hard. "Him talking his way out of trouble at that historical society meeting? I will never forget him all dressed up half-proper, half-scruffy, gangly kid. Everyone else wearing farm clothes and blue jeans and there he's all dressed up, ready to take it like a man and get his just deserts." She wiped a tear away from her eye and brought her voice back down. "Where'd he ever find that hideous tie?"

"I never did know. It wasn't mine. He probably went and bought it special. He's just as proper as they come."

"Except when he's plowing down gravestones."

Mr. L. threw his head back. "Remember that committee meeting, that inquiry panel they held? Like a damn congressional hearing. The poor boy just sitting up straight, listening, serious as can be, trying to make it right."

"Just nodding away. *Yes, sir. No, ma'am.* Just as proper as they come."

"I think he volunteered hisself for about a thousand hours of community service, too."

Norma L. shook her head and held her elbows with opposite hands. "Worked half of them in those gravestones. I've never seen so many holly bushes planted in such a small plot ever before."

"And the bulbs. How many damned paper whites does one cemetery need, anyway?"

She pressed her hand against the middle of her husband's chest, leaning her weight against his, laughing.

They straightened up and didn't bother trying to pick stars through the oaks' leaves that night. Instead they wrapped their arms around each other's waists and approached the door on the first floor together. Norma L. leaned her head on her husband's shoulder, still laughing, still remembering how earnest the kid was through it all.

Mr. L. knocked loudly on the vibrating door.

Nothing happened.

They stood, waiting.

Mr. L. looked at his wife. She shrugged. Then, when a moth came a little too close to her hair, she nodded with decided assertion. So Mr. L. pounded on the door.

The stereo clicked off and the oaks stopped vibrating. The stairs stopped vibrating. The isolation spread out over blue bean fields, turning into sustenance somehow. Mr. and Mrs.

L. couldn't quite hear the moth wings lighting the doorway, with their interminable soft, beating radiance.

Inside the kid maneuvered to the door. They heard him coming. They braced themselves. The trees merged into the sky as the day's last blue drained away. There were metal noises on the other side of the door. Mr. L shut his eyes letting himself merge with the darkness. Norma L. smiled a sort of hesitation and hoped the moths weren't too near her hair.

The door opened and Mr. L's eyes caught right up.

He said, "Hey, kid. Want a bite to eat?"

The kid backed his wheelchair out of the doorway inviting them in. Norma L. propped up her smile first from the edges of the mouth. Finding the effort ineffective, she let her cheeks go and pulled her entire face into a beaming expression of cheery hopefulness by raising her eyebrows. "It's our—well, we just haven't had a chance to cook for you since you've been back.

We thought tonight was as good a night as any. You like pot roast?"

"Pot roast? I knew it. Smelled it cooking all afternoon. Some special kind of dinner, huh? Thought it was Mr. L's birthday. But it was to surprise me?"

Norma nodded.

"Thanks. Thanks a lot, Mrs. L." The kid looked at his stereo and then shifted in his chair. "Does my music ever bother you guys?"

"Not at all. I don't even hear it." She turned to her husband, "Do you ever hear it, dear?"

"Nope. This is an old building. Sturdy. Not thin walls like these new places."

Mrs. L. looked at the kid. "So do you mind if I set this up?"

"Come on in. You know where everything is. It's your house."

They moved toward the table. The kid said, "I'm trying not to nick it. It's so pretty. I stay away from it with the chair. I'm still not a pro in this thing."

Mr. L. said, "Don't worry about the table, kid. It's old as can be. It can take a few lumps."

Down the hall, Mrs. L. found her own mother's favorite tablecloth still folded carefully on an upper shelf in the linen closet. She turned her mind away from the disorder on the lower shelves, where wrinkled towels, half-used bottles of cologne, and well-worn earphones were piled in an accessible jumble behind one slender, hollow door, in a duplex, in a rural patch of woods, in the middle of nowhere. Back in the room, with an over-exerted smile on her face, she spread out the tablecloth, then made several trips up and down the stairs, bringing each dish in turn. The men talked. And since the young man couldn't offer much assistance they concentrated on other proper things in conversation and pretended it was okay not to help with all the carrying a late-middle-aged woman was doing on those wet wooden stairs. They listened to Mrs. L.'s careful progress in her low navy pumps.

The men hovered as Mrs. L. arranged and rearranged the table. The kid said, "It's so pretty. Walnut?"

"Maple."

Mrs. L. carried in the flowers and set them in the middle of the table. She wished she had finished arranging them. She hated their being two heights. She left again, letting one moth in by accident.

Mr. L. said, "A lot of love in that table. My daddy made it when I was a kid. I helped him with some of the finishing work."

The kid lifted the tablecloth and ran his hand across the wood. "Maybe I could make furniture or something."

"Sure you could. The garage is half workshop already. We could make a boardwalk through the oaks over to it. Wouldn't take a weekend to do it. I've seen plenty of boardwalks in state parks now. Makes 'em accessible. I'm sure the plans are online. You could help me figure it."

"I've never really done anything with wood. Just cars or whatever. But it's hard to lean under the hood now. You know? So maybe wood. Pull it onto my lap, right?"

"Yep. You're young yet. Plenty of time to learn." Mr. L. swallowed hard and pinched his waist.

Mrs. L. set plates and pulled off pieces of foil. Besides the pot roast there were mashed potatoes and green beans.

The kid pulled up and slammed his chair against the wood by accident. "I'm so sorry."

"What'd I say, kid?"

Norma said, "The tablecloth will keep it from marking. Don't worry about it, honey. Hand me your plate."

The kid propped up his own smile. He handed her his plate. As she handed it back and both their hands were on it, he said, "It happened in Mosul."

Norma L. let go.

Mr. L. said, "You're home now." Hand on the nearest shoulder.

The flowers and the moth and Mr. and Mrs. L and the kid filled up the room before retracting.

"Your candlesticks are real pretty, Mrs. L."

"Thank you. They were a wedding gift from my Great-Aunt Ginny."

"Yeah?"

"Yeah."

"How long you guys been married?"

"Thirty-eight years tod—thirty-eight years."

"Wow. That's a long time."

The kid put the napkin in his lap. Mrs. L's eyes filled with tears. She stared hard at the uneven flowers, forced the tears into submission, and smiled pleasantly trying not to think her way under the table.

The kid said, "I'm sorry you gotta climb those stairs now, Mr. L. I know your knees are bad."

"My knees are just fine. And it's good for the heart, kid." He looked down at his plate, took up his knife, his fork, sat up as straight as he could, cut the meat, and muttered again. "Good for the heart."

FLAG BOX

A violent, vibrant storm rushed in and then vanished leaving a stupid, ripped flag all tangled in our do-it-yourself rose arbor. The one my wife never felt was a good enough incarnation of her dreams. So I took the neighbor's kid, this cute little girl, to use the flag box in front of the post office. It was a week ago. My wife wouldn't have allowed it. But. She was with our three cats at the vet.

I don't think she'll leave me. She's mentioned it twice in the past eight months. But. Hopefully she's not serious. I think she just wants me to get a job. I want to get a job, too. Her staying or leaving really won't change how fast that happens.

I was a chemist. Sort of. Ran gels in a lab until the grant money disappeared. The other two lab techs got spots in the department. They're involved. They do all the stuff you're supposed to do to keep jobs: play the musical chairs, put in five bucks for birthday cakes, talk to the professors and researchers about hockey. I've never been good at that stuff.

There's a thing, you know. Some kind of guy thing. I don't have it. I'm not queer. Been married for almost twelve years. Just never figured it was worth spending a lot of energy pissing all over each other, jockeying for power or whatever like guys are supposed to do. But sometimes it gets me.

I was talking with my sister last night. We were having a theoretical kind of debate. She said she hates being passive, resents it. I don't know what she's talking about. Except that I hate having to be some kind of hero on a stupid old-time white horse. Like it's my responsibility to stop all the robbers on trains. That's not my business. Why don't they just not rob anybody. Problem solved. Plus, no one's ridden horses in a hundred and twenty years. But. People don't care. They still think I'm supposed to save the day. There's no way I'd rescue the pucker-lipped damsel in distress tied to the tracks, punch out some bad guy, run along the roof jumping from one passenger car to the next while a picturesque steam engine blows whistle shrieks into the desert sky.

I don't know. All I know is I saw my neighbor's kid, a little girl about three years old with gold hair that'll no doubt end up losing its curls and shine, outside. She was dancing in a flag. The storm had been terrible. During the worst of it the flag, a pretty large one maybe four-by-six feet, blew off its pole near the cemetery. It got caught in the rose trellis behind my house. When I first saw her running like a bull through a toreador's cape the sky was still purple. July is like that. The sun on one side gleaming. Dark clouds on the opposite horizon grudgingly moving on.

God, she was having fun.

Okay. Now this little girl next door lives under a strange mix of incoherent rules and inefficient supervision. I don't really look out for her. My wife and this little girl's mother are archenemies. I don't remember why. I tried to block it out while it was happening. Conflict's not my thing. But. My wife is basically right. The mom's kind of a nut. So it's not like I'm babysitting. But. I just kind of make sure this little girl's okay out there—not in the street when cars go by if she's running around out front and not falling down into the ravine if she's spinning in circles out back. I don't even think her mom would notice if she ran into the street or fell in the ravine, you know? But I do know that if I instructed her kid even once that woman would come out of nowhere to hunt me down. I can just see her with her big rack flopping everywhere saying I was way out of line and keep my mouth out of her family business. I don't need that shit. I just think it's stupid to let a kid run wild everywhere. Especially when she's in my yard half the time.

So. I stay away from the mother but me and this little girl became some kind of companions after I lost my job. Nothing dirty. I don't have any weird thing for little girls. But. I make sure she doesn't succumb to an accidental death without anyone noticing. It's good. She gives me hope. Well, hope for a second before I remember no one else much cares. So. I've been known to turn the sprinklers on. To leave new beach balls on the lawn. Most days this summer I've watched her race across my yard. And I won't apologize for it.

Anyway a week ago after the storm that wet flag tangled in the trellis surged. And while the wind whipped the red, white, and blue material the little girl raced under it and around the roses, burst straight into the stripes as the wind switched directions and snapped the flag back. She laughed and screamed one or two of those really self-confident little-girl yelps. I had to smile. The sun shone through the colors and highlighted her damp gold hair as the dark clouds receded slowly taking the big winds with them.

Humidity returned. The sky's contrast drained to hazy gray. Her glorious flapping toy dropped to a deadweight curtain, so suddenly tragic—trapped—after just being so brilliant and bold. As if the little girl knew I'd be watching from the window she whirled on me and demanded help with an intense brown-eyed stare.

She's looked at me like that once or twice in the past. I've always stayed inside to avoid that mouth on the woman next door. But last week I felt as sorry for the little girl as she did for that hung-up flag.

I thought of a lawsuit, of the neighbors worrying unnecessarily about an adult man and their little girl, but no matter how whacked-out her mother can be, the moment mattered more.

I ambled across the yard, kneeled down next to that cute little girl, and awaited my instructions.

"We have to help it." She started to cry and hugged me.

Women. Can't hardly please any of them.

For I don't know how many years my wife went on and on about how she wanted a rose trellis. I don't know what kind of grand scale she felt would be worthy. But she was always pointing out pictures from landscaping books from the library. What was I supposed to do? She's the one who files the tax return. But I did what I could and finally installed one as a surprise on our anniversary.

Shouldn't have bothered. She was immediately disappointed with it. Said the color was wrong. Said it was too rickety. Said the weight of the branches would crush it. Said there was no point growing roses anyway. Threw herself on the bed in a fit of rage because she was too old to start training roses over an arbor in the backyard at this point. But I'd spent a good four hundred dollars on the thing. And paid a guy seventy-five more to dig a few holes, pour some cement, and figure out how to get it propped up. We might not ever live anywhere like that Amalienborg Palace she always talks about going to see but

we're not even close to too old for anything. So I
started the climbing roses myself.

I wasn't thinking about any of that last
week. I was just looking at this little girl with her
lip all pouty not knowing how to help the flag. My
father's voice became mine. "Well, sweetie, look."
I pointed to a corner of the flag which had settled
on the wet grass. "Don't let it touch the ground.
Flags are never to touch the ground."

She leapt to her duty and stood with her
little arms extended far above her head; the flag
wrapped wet around them.

"I'll get the ladder, and we'll get it down,"
I said.

It's not quick, you know. But my roses
climbed that trellis just fine. You just tie the
branches to it as they grow. That's it. And the
color of the thing doesn't matter at all. During the
summer you can hardly see an inch of it anymore.
And it's not gonna collapse either. Stood up in a
storm that tore a flag right off its pole, didn't it?

I came back with the ladder but forgot my
gloves. For twenty minutes I wrestled with the

rose branches' long, fat thorns. Ensnared material was everywhere because the wind had changed directions so many times. But when I felt like shirking my duty even long enough to just go get the gloves—let alone a big pair of scissors that really would have expedited the process—I'd see that little girl's frame with arms still extended earnestly, with full trust about my words that the flag should never touch the ground. So I worked on. My wet skin burned from the scratches. I looked down at her. "This might take a while. Won't your mother wonder where you are?" She was reverent and stayed silent, her head under the makeshift tent. She reached higher. I saw her little fingers adjust their grip.

I shook my head. "Okay. If you say so."

But damn I wanted those gloves and that pair of scissors.

Finally I extracted the thing and held it. Together we stood near the trellis and the ladder holding the heavy wet flag off the ground.

She started to get tired, whined just slightly, "What now?"

How should I know? Folding the flag while taps played on a beat-up old trumpet couldn't be arranged quickly enough to give an exhausted three-year-old a ritual tribute.

My arms were poked full of thorn holes and burning. I rubbed my hairy forearm with a couple wide fingers. Whistled low, forcing air through my teeth, buying time.

She kicked at mosquitoes.

I said, "Well, now we take it to the flag box!"

"The flag box?"

"Yeah. They have one in front of the post office. It's where you put old flags."

I put the ladder back and let her pick a special flag container from all the stuff in my shed. We didn't ask for permission to go or really even think of it in the moment. Her mom would have said no for little reason.

I drove carefully but let her ride in the front seat. I think it was a first for her. All these child safety laws with the car seats, you know. But. It was important that she sit right next to me as an equal. The flag lay between us in a wooden apple crate.

She kept one hand on it.

We rode through wet streets in silence. When we got to the post office I showed her the flag box, a converted blue street-side mail drop-box painted red, white, and blue with stars and stripes. I said, "The American Legion puts these boxes out so they can collect and dispose of the flags in an honorable way."

"What's the 'merican Legion?"

I've never been quite sure myself. "They help out with flags and they probably fought in a war."

She listened. And waited, thinking.

I hoped she wouldn't ask me what flags have to do with war. She didn't. She said, "What do they do with the flags?"

I had no idea. They probably burned them in a ceremonious rite. I just knew they handled all the pomp and circumstance required for caretaking flags. "They make sure the stars find eyes to sleep in and the stripes go on end to end from here to California."

She nodded.

I held the flag off the ground while she readied her step. After the apple crate was steady she climbed onto it. I opened the little door and held the back of the flag while she stuffed and shoved and pushed the material into the box.

I tried not to think of mildew. Surely the American Legion folks check the box often. "Not to worry." They seemed the sort.

She kissed the last corner of the flag good-bye, letting her fingers loosen one by one. When the last bit slipped away I let the slot's door snap shut.

TANDEM

Going back in time and forward too, they drove across the western edge of the Eastern Time Zone and lost an hour. A carol recording played too loudly into the landscape at a Christmas tree farm in 2006. It was almost dark. The scent of hot spiced cider and gingerbread cookies came down from the barn where two matronly Midwesterners sat on folding chairs selling wreaths and centerpieces.

In the parking lot the Watsons' dog Squally ran ahead into the rows of evergreen trees, rummaging with her snout, discovering everything she could about the farm's firs and pines as the temperature continued to drop. A frozen crust of what hadn't melted during the warm part of the week covered rutted rows. Dan stopped at the edge of the lane and leaned against a post. "Damn." One boot sole was separating from the leather.

Marie moved on with her head bent down into the wind, following Squally's caprices. She had told him not to wear the boots. She stopped again and folded her arms across her chest. Her red turtleneck sweater and down vest weren't quite warm enough. She should have worn another layer. "Come on, honey." And she really wished she had a hat.

"But the boots. What about Dad's boots?" Catching up to her, whistling sharply for Squally to come back and stay closer, Dan fished through the pockets of his canvas coat and found an old black stocking hat. He handed it to his wife. "They're falling apart."

She did not think to thank him for the hat but held a bright-colored nylon leash, dingy from a year of use, in her hand and decided not to use it. She watched Squally bound off into the trees with pricked ears.

"Why aren't you saying anything? Didn't you hear me?"

Dan held a handsaw at arm's length and swung it in wide arcs almost like the pendulum dips of an amusement park's Viking ship ride which swings back and forth, up and down, hesitating at the heights before plunging down, releasing joyous screams of terror.

Marie looked at her husband who was walking awkwardly, trying to prevent more mud from getting inside his sock. "Those boots are probably forty years old! You're surprised they're falling apart?" She pulled the hat over the tops of her ears and looked at her own boots. Three hundred muddy dollars.

They got away from the tinny carol.

It was the eighth year of their marriage. Five years before Dan might have said, "Why didn't you put Squally on the leash? They don't want our dog running wild out here." But he just kept walking between the trees, swinging the handsaw and whistling *fweeee!* when Squally got too far away.

The smell of gingerbread was gone.

Dan could not resist. "The kids should be here."

"They're too little and they're both sick, Dan. Why make sick kids ride three hours back in the car, cold, dirty, and wet?"

"Don't you believe in tradition?"

She shook her head. "It was a tradition for your family, Dan. Not mine."

Christmas trees ran in different-sized rows in all directions.

He whistled for Squally again and grabbed the leash out of Marie's gloved hand. He knew what she was probably thinking—that an artificial tree like her mom's would be fine. But her mother's tree looked like a department store display. It was an eyesore of enormous bows, doves, angels. "Shake that self-righteous head all you want, Marie. But there will be no fake trees in my house. Ever."

She watched him clip Squally's collar and wrap most of the length around his hand. "Fine. But who was seven months pregnant last Christmas on the floor with the watering can getting needles in my eyes trying to keep that twelve-foot monstrosity alive, Dan? That thing drank a gallon of water a day. It filled two vacuum bags with needles in the first week. And was it you under that tree trying to keep it alive for six weeks? No, it was not."

"You always exaggerate." Dan kept Squally close, swung the old oiled saw absentmindedly from his other hand, and walked into one of the rows of blue spruce. "That was not a twelve-foot tree. We don't even have twelve-foot ceilings."

Marie waited in the lane until Dan was a good twenty feet ahead. She watched the distance increasing between them.

Squally barked, calling Marie forward into the row. It was that familiar friendly yip, the same sweet, clipped bark Squally used to announce that the baby's bottle had fallen out of the stroller, clattery plastic on concrete, rolling down the sidewalk. Still irritated with her husband, Marie picked her steps carefully in his footprints, keeping her boots as clean as possible.

They moved silently between the trees.

Marie could stop, scream, demand the keys, cry, insist on leaving, go sit in the car, take the dog off the leash again. But she didn't. She caught up to him. "Well, it was nine feet anyway. A nine-foot freaking monstrosity that put me into debt just to decorate." She pulled Squally's leash back into her possession.

The dog meandered along the full demonstrable generosity of leash length.

Dan's left foot was soaked inside the boot. He lifted his toes to protect them from the worst. This compensation added complexity to his gait. "Well, nobody died and made you Martha Stewart, Marie. You could have just spread out the decorations we had instead of drenching every single branch and then filling up the whole storage space with that overpriced tacky-ass shit."

"It's not tacky. It's Radko." She kept
following Dan, giving Squally a tug. "Isn't there a
Christmas tree farm closer to Chicago, Dan?
Driving three hours is ridiculous."

"Every tree my whole life has come from
this farm. I don't care if I have to drive ten hours;
every year, every tree, as long as I can manage it,
will come from this tree farm."

"And I'm self-righteous?" She tried not to
think permanently-disabling thoughts about her
husband. Why did they go through this every
year? For what? For a Christmas tree? It was fine
before the kids were born, kind of quaint, but
now? They worked overtime all week. They still
had a ton of shopping to finish, mostly to keep
from hearing some litany of dissatisfaction from
his mother. The old boots? The traditional tree
farm? He was unbearable when he got like this—a
nostalgic romantic who just would not let things
go.

Marie unclipped Squally and watched the
dog's silky coat ripple as she ran full force after a
cardinal. "All this back-to-your-roots stuff gets

old. There is no reason for us to drive all the way down here every year when the trees they sell right by us come from a bunch of farms just like this one. Your hick-ass, Puritanical bullshit only goes so far, Dan."

Dan shouted toward the sunset. "Squally!"

The dog disappeared into the darkening evening.

Marie pulled off a glove and felt the nearest branches.

An old man in insulated coveralls walked up to them from an adjacent row. "Finding everything, folks?" He kept a straight face and noticed Marie touching the trees. He forgave her unconsciously.

She winced and did not look at him. "You have any that don't drop needles?" It was caustic but not quite rude.

He ignored the tone. "We sure do. Scotch pine will do pretty good that way. I salvaged a few during the blight. Care if we drive out to the rows? It's too far for me to walk anymore."

Dan nodded his interest in the man's suggestion and ostentatiously took his wife by the hand.

They followed the old man to his truck, which was parked at an angle on a nearby rise.

He turned to Dan. "My eyes aren't so great with the light this low. Mind if I ride and you drive? It's a four-on-the-floor." He was not asking. He had already walked around to the passenger side and was helping Marie up into the truck. He closed the passenger side door and settled himself against it.

"It's been a while since I drove a stick." Dan put the saw in the bed of the truck, lowered the tailgate, and whistled.

"This old beast has had more clutches than I've had chicken dinners. Don't worry about grinding the gears. She can take it."

Squally came running and jumped up into the bed of the truck, an old pro at a new trick. She settled down to drowse on a tarp between the spare tire and the saw. Dan got into the driver's seat.

The old man watched Marie struggling to get comfortable between the two men and with the gearshift rising out of the floor of the truck. He said, "Now, I'm sorry, I didn't catch your name."

"Marie."

Slowly, emphasizing every single word, the old man said, "Okay. Now, Marie. I realize that this may not be the way you are used to riding. But I will tell you that most hick-ass women are not as Puritanical as you might think."

Marie flushed. "Excuse me?"

"There's not a one of them that doesn't know how to ride in the middle of a pickup."

Marie was nervous but trusted the laugh lines rooted deep at the edge of the old man's eyes. "I don't understand."

The old man looked out to the horizon and gave his instructions casually to the window. Letting his words make fog on the glass, he said, "Well, and I mean this with the utmost respect, dear. But you have got to straddle that thing and lean up against your husband so he can get to that shifter."

Marie's head snapped. She looked at Dan with wide eyes.

Dan shrugged, mouthing the words, "I don't know. It's his truck."

Marie managed to convince her designer jeans and her yes-I've-had-two-babies legs to straddle the gearshift. She let her left thigh rest against Dan's. She kept her right thigh from ever touching the old man's coveralls.

"Good. Now, Dan—wasn't it Dan?—just ease her back off this little embankment and take us up this lane about two hundred yards."

Dan put his hand over Marie's, who tried to hold onto his fingers with her gloves. He squeezed and let go. In the bed of the truck, Squally stood up, turned around twice, and lay back down again, contented by the truck's motion.

The old man looked at Marie and said, "You got any kids, Marie?"

Of course she had kids. Who doesn't have kids? She pressed her thigh against Dan's, encouraging him to relax and stop grinding the gears. "Two. The oldest is twenty-seven months. And the baby was born at the end of February."

"Good thing you didn't bring them. They'd catch their death out here today at those ages."

Marie leaped to the defensive. "Well, it was a tradition in Dan's family. So we would have brought them if we lived any closer."

"Bring them in a few years after they know all about Santie Claus. Then they'll never forget it." The old man nodded, agreeing with himself. "Go ahead and put it in third, Dan. Nothing to worry about out here. If you hit a deer, you won't even feel it. Truck's high-gauge steel. A regular tank. Drive as fast as you want. Hell. Open her up. We'll come back for the tree. Take us up to my property line at that strip of oaks."

Dan pressed his forearm against Marie's thigh while dropping the truck down into third and then fourth.

They passed well-maintained signage: *Norway Spruce, Serbian Spruce, Concolor Fir, West Coast Noble Fir.* The old man wasn't looking at the signs that marked the rows. He scrutinized the fence line as they bumped past it. Then all three—and Squally probably, too—watched the rushing fence posts. Keeping a keen eye out for any having fallen.

The old man turned back to Marie. "What tradition?"

Marie looked to Dan for approval to tell his story. Dan nodded, paying attention to the drive, loving the speed, loving the sound of frozen grasses shattering under the chassis.

"Dan used to come here, to your farm, every year when he was little. With his dad."

"Wasn't my farm then. I got this place five years ago in a foreclosure settlement."

Dan looked over. "Foreclosure? I thought you worked for the Loftons."

"Nope. At the worst of the blight this place just about got bulldozed for a housing development. Instead the Loftons held on as long as they could. Let the developers fish someone else's place over on 114. By the time they'd fought that fight they were so overextended that they couldn't make the property taxes. I got the place real cheap from the bank."

"But you always farmed around here?"

"No, ma'am. Not me. I was in real estate in Dayton for thirty-four years. I was married right after I got back from Korea. We had three kids: one smart one who can't keep a job for all his politics; one dumb one who can't keep her mouth shut but to say yes to any man dumber than her who comes along; and one who drives an old school bus from one art fair to another every summer and somehow manages to make a living painting hearts, flowers, and smiley faces on tiny wooden beads. Could have been a god-damned surgeon with steady hands like that—but nope, has to paint blessed beads."

Marie looked back into the bed of the truck to check on Squally. The happy mutt gave a cinnamon wag while watching the fence posts zip by under the dark blue broken clouds.

"Don't ask me why I did any of it." The man in coveralls rubbed the inside of the windshield with his sleeve and turned on the defrost blowers. "After I retired I had a charter-fishing boat business in Florida. But even in a subdivided paradise my wife hated me and made my life a living hell for as long as she walked this earth. No American dream for me, Marie. Not for me. Even though I edged my sidewalks clean and pretty in three damn states."

The oak trees held onto dry brown leaves. They all stared into the darkening woods. Dan downshifted and the truck stopped at the property line.

The old man cracked the window again. "I guess I could have divorced her somewhere along the line. Or she could have divorced me. Or something. But that's not what we did. We stuck it out. Did the best we could."

Marie said, "Sounds like you did great."

The old man laughed. "Some old milk slogan used to say, 'Good as any, better than some.' That was us. Good as any, better than some."

Marie was worried. "So you're all alone now? You're way out here by yourself?"

"No, no, no, sweetie. I moved up here with my girlfriend. Buying this place was her idea."

Dan sort of snorted. "Girlfriend?"

"Sure. In Florida, after my wife died, I'd get real bored. Go down to the marina and tinker around on that damned charter boat and end up at that little bar they had there. Me and the other geezers all afternoon. Talking about mangled manatees. What to do about oil leaking into the channel. Whether to charge fathers for little puking kids losing rods overboard—shit like that."

Marie reminded him. "But what about this girlfriend?"

"Elaine? She never lost a rod. She wears a fishing belt. She's no fool."

"I mean, how'd you meet her?"

"Oh, she ran a bait shop on the landing and sold beer and candy and cigarettes, too. She ran the deliveries to the bar in a motorboat. Somehow, I got to helping her unload that motorboat on her runs." The old man sat up straight.

The light was gone. The day was over.

After a long silence, the old man said, "Guess I didn't know about me hating my wife and my wife hating me while she was alive. Guess I thought all that antagonism, all that animosity, all that manipulation and the rest was love. How could I have known different? All those years should've meant something, right?"

"You didn't love your wife?" Marie folded her hands in her lap smoothing the finger of the glove over her wedding ring.

"Not like I love Elaine. Not like that."

The tradition was to implement a pattern that was a kind of suffering self-loathing to which any good person gets humbly indoctrinated. The tradition was to keep doing what you had always known how to do, to give up certain hopes for the someone whose role model said to love you. So what if you'd sacrificed almost everything on a little cross around your neck pulled side to side for years on end?

Marie turned to the old man. "What would you have done different?" She wasn't really asking to know.

"Nothing."

Dan said, "Nothing?" Dan looked back to be sure Squally was still there and not too cold. The dog was asleep.

The old man countered, "Good as any, better than some." He realized how late it was getting. "It's pretty dark to be picking Christmas trees now." But the old man wasn't sentimental. He wasn't a traditionalist. To him it was neither here nor there. He was a businessman. He motioned toward the darkness. "Well, you saw this place. Rows upon rows upon rows. And they're all the same anyway. Hell, we even spend the whole spring pruning so they're every one the damned same, exactly the same. I'll give you one of the precut Scotch pines half-price. No needles in the carpet this year, Marie. There's a six-foot beauty up there if Elaine hasn't sold it. It's plenty fresh."

Marie nodded, holding back tears. The tradition, Dan's tradition which kept the old man's heat on, was to walk into the unknown if familiar rows and pick your own tree, cut it down, carry it out any way you knew how, and call it yours until it died, until it was time, until it was time to let it go.

Throughout the evening the symmetric snowdrifts against the barbed wire fence changed from white to pink to lavender to purple-shadowed hillocks to blue to black and then back to white in the headlight beams.

The truck started up and Dan finally remembered how to drive in the country. He handled the old tank with surety. Marie watched him shifting gears between her legs. Squally must

have woken up as they bounced and lurched over
the frozen ruts.

MY CHAMBERED NAUTILUS

Haven't you begun to believe

in the twisting fate of this wet

world? Always between building

up, breaking free, and starting

again. That's love swim, you know,

you and me beginning.

Brown striped cream. Your hair,

your skin and eyes. And I

watched with such admiration as

you neatly sewed the bubble day's

film onto the walls of your

circle world. You take such care

with the sunshine of things.

People may be barnacle fools and

cut your feet with their parasite

quick kind of (open close open)

habit world, eating their surroundings.

Snatching up the world's

fastest times and making

your irregular life so hard.

But you have moved on again, haven't

you? On to the next little room.

I can't imagine in there with you

learning me. I can only see the

afterward. Broken open and dry.

But I'll bet it's all fleshy pink

joy, inside. Filling up new

between the getting-harder walls.

Boys and girls have nothing

thoughts between them all the

time. You know. Just like us.

And there is slippery understanding

there, in the Between, and the Around,
and the

Just-where-you-can't-quite-reach place.

And then I begin to know a you having

nothing to do with me. A you so

resolute and confined. A you still opening

in tolerable nacre carrels, which harbor

your broad Everything.

No such skin for any of it. Spirals; or

words falling short from the way

It all could be. And then that's

good enough for a while.

I'm washing the dishes and

listening to a bit

of the evening

news on a Tuesday, I think.

PIETA

Solutions come easily when you cradle your dead son on your lap. More strict less strict understanding tolerant easygoing lots of hugs. There aren't any gray areas anymore. I know what I should have done for Jason, what I could have done for him. But it wasn't so easy when he came home drunk, so self-righteous, and so full of hard-edged life. I'd never admit it. Not even to my husband, Dan, but in my mind I called my son Genghis Khan. Because to have this massively disrespectful adult-sized child in my kitchen, with my collections of Longaberger baskets and antique swan figurines, was just beyond

comprehension. I got so sick of his back talk. I
wanted to beat the insolent belligerence out of
him. Don't get me wrong; I never hit my child,
but I did as much with words. Well not me,
exactly. My husband was the enforcer.

I never questioned it. Because other
people's children tiptoe in and try to sleep off
their beers. Not my son. Seventeen, eighteen,
nineteen, curfews didn't matter. He'd come into
the house with an armload of empty beer bottles
and dump them in my kitchen trash can. He never
got sick; just wanted to eat. Invariably he'd cook
something. Two in the morning and he'd have
half the kitchen torn apart trying to make
scrambled eggs or grilled cheese and bacon.
Never anything simple like a bowl of cereal.

Upstairs I'd roll over and fret. My mind
was in a constant tizzy about whether we should
have done more of this or that. Everything that
seemed like it might have been a mistake replayed
to haunt me. Regret is not a strong enough word.
I was dismantled. Night after night the world I
tried to build came down. And it was never meant

to be a dungeon for him, never a cell he was sentenced to as punishment. I wanted a fortress just to protect him, to keep him safe, to give him a chance. Because I knew no one would understand. People wouldn't love him like I did if they knew the truth. Maybe we'd been keeping secrets from him about some part of life he should have understood. But how could he know anything about what I did? He wasn't even born.

But that kid picked up on something. When he'd come home all clattering beer bottles like that, it's not that Dan and I weren't already awake waiting for him every time. We were usually in bed each pretending the other might be sound asleep. After twenty minutes of listening to dishes break and cans of corned beef hash fall on the tile, to the faucet running to overflowing and him banging around into everything, it was like a pattern. I'd say, "Maybe I should just go down and make him a real meal." Only after my suggestion did the man I married ever say, "No. No. You get some sleep, dear."

No one knew. Jason didn't look much different from his brother. But. Oh God. What I wouldn't do to have those three weeks of my life back. Dan forgave me, let me come home, and that was it. We moved on with our lives. Did everything we could for both our sons.

But Dan operated from this frightening sense of honor about the whole thing. So those nights when Jason came home drunk, when I was about to get up and go down to him, maybe even sit with him long enough to tell the whole story, my husband always did what he thought was the right thing. Dealt with it for me, you know? So he'd pat me and go downstairs. Exactly the same way every time. "No. No. You get some sleep, dear." And then two taps like I might have been a Labrador.

And that was it. Dan kicked off the covers, muttered, swore a bit to me, and went downstairs. He always started in on him the same way. "Damn it, Jason. Your mother is trying to sleep. What the hell do you think you're doing actin' a fool in my house? Are you drunk?"

Now even if me and my husband had a routine upstairs Jason had two different responses. He'd either laugh hysterically and go right on bumpin' into things, or he'd fly into an uncontrollable rage. Personally, I liked the rage better. They got everything out in the open. Sure they fought like hell. I half-thought they'd like to kill each other some of those nights. But they got exhausted quick and stormed off to bed within the hour.

If Jason laughed right in his father's face, though, those nights took a lot longer. Instead of screaming fits I heard taunting, jeering, and lectures. I never went down, but I could just see my Dan standing in the middle of our kitchen with his hands on his hips and his spindly little-old-man legs running down into those disreputable slippers, seething mad at the insolence, professing his infinite knowledge to the drunk cook. All the while I could hear Jason disrespecting his father, darting all around in the cabinets and the pantry looking for different things to throw into his late-night snack. Once they went on that way for more than three hours.

In the morning I'd clean up an incredible mess. There'd be the skillet with eggs, tomatoes, cheese, even chocolate chips cooked up and stuck to my Teflon.

Sometimes, instead of saying anything to my husband in our bedroom, I'd try to get to my son first. I'd get up and make a motion to go down before Dan so I could talk to Jason alone, make a little peace, maybe sedate him some. But I never made it farther than the landing. I guess it was a father-son time. Really those nights were about the only time those two were ever in the same room together. Jason avoided his father. Dan just seemed oblivious to his older son a lot of the time. He gets along better with Daniel. I try not to notice. Dan tries not to have it be true.

I wish I wouldn't have been so apprehensive those nights. I could have marched down the stairs like Cleopatra and told them both to go straight to hell or at least suggest they see some kind of psychologist. I knew there was something wrong, but I didn't know how to help. Guess it was the guilt, the shame. And just not believing that three weeks in a life matters much at all. If it was happening to anyone else's kid, I would have had all the answers. You can see it better. You've got the distance, the perspective, to know what might help. But you can't say a word. Can't judge. No one can. So I acted like an idiot with my own son. I flashed him sappy smiles or reached out to touch him as he jerked away. I don't know. I used to think he favored me. But I don't know now. Maybe in some ways he didn't respect me as much as he did his father. That's probably why I never told him. He would have hated me, judged me, judged himself.

But he should have known his story. And there were times, dark times, lonely times, boring times in my life when just looking at my son gave me so much joy. Because he was a reminder of those three amazing weeks. He had the same shape head as his real father. And sometimes when I'd sit in my chair next to Dan, watching the news or a movie in the evening with the kids, I'd just look at the shape of Jason's head and be transported to a place that made me smile. I couldn't live without Dan. But that child was a true blessing to me his whole life.

Still. I don't know if he respected anything. I guess he liked that job delivering milk and ice cream. He knew every one of the restaurant, convenience store, and gas station owners and managers in a forty-mile radius. Liked his boss. Liked training the new guys. Ran two routes a day when someone was out sick or if one of the guys' wives was having a baby.

I fell into a habit of doing things for him that I remembered he liked when he was little. Stupid, I know. I baked cookies and left him little notes on the kitchen table like I used to. I hope it comforted him a bit. He was having such a rough time in those years. With cancer patients—my mother died of cancer—at least you can dope them up on painkillers. You know they're suffering and there's something you can do for them. But there is so little you can do for someone like my Jason. It was just as chronic. I remember thinking that I was glad he drank because maybe it would numb some of that pain in his little lover-shaped head. I never said that to Dan. It's absurd to even think drinking's the answer. Most people would call me crazy. I think I was right, though.

But then I was just holding him there in the street. I knew I should have told him everything, should have defended my son to Dan, to the world.

I never could.

I remember how I heard the screech and how the transformer popped right before the electricity went out. Dan was on a business trip. I ran through the garden in my robe. I remember it felt like I was wearing a bedsheet. The cotton was too crisp and wouldn't move fast enough.

The car was smashed in on the passenger's side and the pole he hit had fallen. Electric lines hung slack and one was broken. Its two limp sinister ends swung slowly. I couldn't find him at first. Had to be careful of those live wires. I looked in the car, but he wasn't there.

Usually Victoria's security light floods three acres. But Jason hit whatever pole controlled that. I knew she'd make a call so I just kept running, looking everywhere.

There was a moon. It was that slack moon that always makes me uneasy, wishing for the beauty of phases that are more or less full. But thank God for the light of that slumped thing in the sky or I never would have found him.

He was thrown across the road. Almost into a ditch on the other side. He was so blue-white in that light. It made him look dead the minute I saw him. It was odd. You imagine a body just lying nice and flat, but he was all crumpled up. His right arm stuck straight out, falling down the slope of the new spring grass. His left arm must have broken because it just sank where something should have been bone. His left foot was on the road, but his right foot was way up under his chest.

His beautiful face got crushed half-slack just like that sorry moon. His head was twisted, his neck obviously broken, his mouth open with

the top row of teeth sunk into the gravel and mud
on the shoulder of the road. His tongue was
hanging down in it. God. I sat there with his head
in my lap for maybe fifteen minutes. Probably
shorter than that, really. It was pitch black except
for the moon and the stars.

Those so-called sweet birdies chuck their
young out of the nest and if they can't fly—oh
well. Can those parents possibly know? Do they
have an instinct about when their chick is ready to
fly? We didn't. Not really. We just figured by the
time he was as old as he was he should be able to
hack it.

Oh, I knew everything for a moment.
Everything about teaching responsibility and self-
respect and obligation and fear. Sitting in that
gravel, trying to lift his whole weight onto my lap,
unable, and then with his crushed skull in my
hands, like I could fix it, maybe, but no, as soon
as he wasn't so vividly alive, I had answers. I gave
myself pompous advice, came up with solutions
about what to do with truth and lies. Dan goes to

church a lot now I've noticed, but it doesn't help
me much.

SHOULD: HOW MOMMY ATE HER SOUL

There are more than 2000 hash marked lines on the beltway between my house and work. I get off at 5 a.m. and the only way I seem to get home is by staring at the hash marks off my left front fender. I count them and I stay to the right of them.

I don't mind my job. I work nights at a security booth for a gated community. The pay is ridiculously good for the work, because the community residents place such a pompous regard on getting into their community. They value my ability to keep people out. But I don't keep anyone out. The gate does.

There are two hundred gated communities in town. If anyone really wants to get into a gated community to kill people in their sleep, rape and pillage the women and children, steal the pool table imported from Italy, or drive really fast up and down the streets being obnoxious, most likely they will do it somewhere else. My job is easy.

Mostly I get huge tips from high school kids to write down a time in the log book ten minutes before they were supposed to be home. Some nights I'm convinced the parents moved to the gated community just for the log book. A third party to settle disputes. More often than not in the early morning there comes a mother in a silk robe driving an SUV. It screeches to a halt behind my booth, and she shuffles up in slippers to scrutinize my entries for the past twelve hours. I don't mind. I like the kids. But kids shouldn't be tipping that kind of money. And no woman who's a mother should be wearing that kind of robe.

More often than not after midnight there is no one. And I sleep.

If I can't sleep I look out the glass and stare at the gated community's sewage irrigation fountain. Every community has one. A little pond. A pretty fountain. A sign not to swim or fish.

If I am asleep it is the sound of Mr. Hawthorne's running shoes which wakes me. He lives at the back of the community, 10974 Eagle's Wake Trail, Hawthorne M & N. He runs to the front of the neighborhood and then stretches near the pond. My last duty before I am relieved by the computer is to release Mr. Hawthorne into the world for his run.

He is gray-haired and sweet. He always smiles as he goes and shouts, "Thanks Annie!" with an arm thrown up to the sky.

"Ann. Ann!"

I'm sitting in the garage, in my car. I can hear my husband calling. His voice holds so much. He thinks he'll be late. He's convinced that it's my fault. He was up all night with one of the kids or the baby. If I was any kind of mother I would have been the one there for them. After all they were calling for me not him. He can't find the shoes he wants to wear. He forgot to pick up the dry-cleaning so he doesn't have the shirt he wants. If I was any kind of wife I would be the one ironing. There's no food because no one went shopping this weekend because we had to go to that stupid christening/wedding/high school graduation party/50th anniversary celebration/work picnic/Christmas gala and why should I miss the game just to get groceries?

Him calling me says all of this and more. It doesn't always say *I missed you, I still love you, I need you to work so we can pay for the tree house that we bought on credit and then destroyed in the assembly process.* And it never says, "Welcome Home, Dear. Did you have a good day at work?"

I don't tell my husband about my tips. The tips go to the lunch room at Chateau Neuf with me alone. I thought once about taking Katrina my oldest girl for some special mommy time. But I knew her sweet innocence would

reveal all to her father. So I let her have special
time with him and I keep Chateau Neuf for me.

I hear myself say, "Welcome Home, Dear.
Did you have a good day at work?"

"You would never believe these assholes."

His voice trails off as he walks down the
hall. He keeps talking for two hours from this
point. Every day.

It's not that I don't care about his work. I
guess I do. I certainly should.

At the first hour into his monologue there
always comes a single line. It doesn't vary much
from this:

"If I got a decent night's sleep once in
while I could handle it."

We settle onto the couch. We turn on the
TV.

What my husband doesn't realize is that
for all he knows I don't sleep. He has never seen
me at work. He must assume I am working. And
yet he never sees me sleep at home. So the gall of
him even uttering this line in my presence is

unbearable. I hear myself say, "I suppose so, honey."

There is one woman who comes to my booth almost every night. She wears her robe and slippers. She comes with a thermos and a radio and a deck of cards. Her husband is having an affair and her children never obey their curfew. She sits with me in my booth and we have a great time. She watches them pull through the gate. She writes down the time and then we play cards until she passes out in a heap on the cement floor. She has an air mattress that she stows in my cubby booth. Rarely does she bother to inflate it. When she does it fills up the entire booth. She sits on it like a chair with part on the floor and part going up the wall where the door is. It is hysterical. She always brings her stainless steel thermos. Sometimes she brings coffee but more often it is filled with white Godiva liqueur, Kahlúa and three cups of vodka over ice. She calls her thermos the Stealth Bomber.

We laugh a lot about the thermos.

I have never known her name. Her address is 12488 Peregrine Falcon Lane. Her husband is William F. Fessner. She told me once that she kept her maiden name. But she never told me what it was. Interesting. I worry sometimes that I will read in the paper that a certain woman has committed suicide. It will be her and I will never know from her name.

Duty begins this way all the time: I am on the couch, reading a magazine in a moment of peace. The front door opens. Two feet stamp away the slush collected from his effort to make it to the mailbox and back before coming inside.

HOLSTERS IN THE GUESTROOM

Roni'd been cleaning, breastfeeding her son, and wiping dog slobber off the floor for the better part of the day. When her son vomited breast milk all over both himself and her, she was already running late to pick up her husband's college friend from the South Shore. Roni changed the baby's clothes, put him in his swing, jumped in and out of the shower for thirty seconds, threw on her husband's old FBI SWAT training tee shirt, put her five-month-old son into his carrier, and grabbed her keys. "Jesus Christ," she said under her breath but didn't stumble on the guitar that her dog must have knocked down again with his big wagging tail.

She pulled her wet hair up, picked up her son in his bulky, crash-test-rated car seat, dragged it through three rooms, shoved her feet into some old wedge flip-flops, and rushed through the laundry room toward the garage.

She tried to think about what she'd say to Brandon's friend. She couldn't remember if this was the guy that ended up going to the police academy at the same time as Brandon or if this guy worked with her husband at the stromboli place for five years. She should know. So she couldn't ask. Maybe she could ask him whether he had any good stories on Brandon from when they first met. She definitely wanted to clarify which guy this was before she got back to the house to make their dinner.

Either way she was about to miss his train if she didn't hurry. Hopefully she could catch mostly green lights on the way there and be at the front of the line of cars picking up commuters. She hurried to the garage steps as best she could while lugging the awkward baby carrier because she hated being in the back of that Kiss & Ride line more than she hated being in a rush to leave the house. But at the foot of the garage stairs she just stopped.

Her navy sedan was backlit with blinding light off the cement. The garage door gaped.

She gripped the handle of the baby carrier but didn't look down at her son. All the motion and momentum that had gathered in the past ten minutes dissipated to nothing. It wasn't even worth hesitating. She took the first step and stood on the second step of the garage stairs overwhelmed by both knowledge and disbelief. It took brute force to move up one more step and stand immobilized on the third shocked but not surprised. She stared into the backseat of her car.

She didn't hope. She didn't pray. She just said to herself, "I really don't need this right now." She climbed the last step and stood on the garage floor. She shifted the heavy car seat from one side of her body to the other. Her son kicked his feet in the carrier, treaded socks in the air.

Brandon's friend's train was due to arrive in ten minutes. But it didn't matter. What choice did she have? She had to deal with this bullshit again. She set her son's carrier down on top of a fifty-pound bucket of dog food and sent a text to her mom: *What happened?*

Then she walked around to the other side of the car to be sure.

Her husband's motorcycle lay tipped over on the pile of recycling.

Yep.

God damn it.

The driver's side passenger door was standing wide open and her father lay passed out in the backseat.

Roni felt nothing. She just wanted her dad out of her car. She wanted him not there at all. Inert like the mountain bikes, the garden hose, the lawn seed spreader, the broken fire pit, the black shelving, the bag of bulb fertilizer, the snow shovel, the weed whacker, the new wagon, and the crib box, she just blinked. She didn't cry. She didn't scream. She didn't throw anything. She didn't abandon her son. She didn't kick the aging, tyrannic bastard.

She said, "Dad. Wake up. Get out of my car. I need to go. I need to be somewhere."

He didn't move.

She pushed her dad's knee gently but firmly by shutting the car door against his shins. He didn't notice. She picked up each of his legs and let them drop. They were deadweight. She poked him in the chest. He was nearly lifeless— didn't respond to any stimulus. She tried to drag him out of the car but he was too big. She had trouble enough lugging her son around. There was no way she could move her father. It was an exercise in futility to even push isometrically against the accumulated weight, resistance, and friction of their intolerant years. She tried to shove her dad into the car but his clothes against the upholstery of her car seat created too much drag for her to overcome.

Her son started to cry.

She looked over at him, balanced there in a plastic safety device on the dog food. What was she even trying to protect him from? She hadn't noticed any of the dog food scattered across the concrete floor, or that raccoons had likely been in her garage. Her recycling was chewed up and torn. There were scat pellets. So then she did feel something. Not disappointment, rage, or aggression having anything to do with her father's being so exhaustingly who he was. No. She was infuriated that the garage door had been open all night and that wild animals got into her dog's food.

She walked around the car to the big bucket of dog food and started rocking her son. He fell asleep fairly easily. She moved him off the dog food container and put him in the middle of the hood of her car. She got a blue-handled broom and dustpan to clean up what she could. She sprayed urine remover in all the places she found scat.

Her mother texted her back about what had happened with her father last night.

Roni read her mother's explanation but did not respond. Instead, she texted her husband to say that she was going to miss his friend's train. She gave no explanation to her husband, just told him to text his friend and let him know.

Her husband was livid and responded right away. He said, no, he wasn't going to text his friend, that she just needed to go and pick him up, that there was no reason for her to be late, she was just sitting around all day, and that it's not like his friend can just call a taxi—it'd cost a fortune if any ghetto cab even did show up. Her husband's follow-up text said that he never should have given her any responsibility and that he knew she didn't like his even having friends but that she had no right to leave the poor guy hanging.

She did not cry. She did not call her husband at work to scream at him about her father's lying passed out drunk in the backseat of her car. She did not throw her phone down and stamp on it. She did not call her friend to get the name of that divorce lawyer.

She absorbed what she could and did nothing.

After twenty-nine years of listening to all her mother's excuses she was not about to explain anything about this to her husband. She was too sick of all the reasons why. She did not respond to her husband at all. She just looked at her son on the hood of the car to be sure he'd be okay there for another minute and disappeared into the house. She returned with a plastic cup of water, walked around to the rear passenger door, and threw the water in her father's face.

He blinked. He spit. She was patient and maybe a little afraid when she told her dad to just pull his feet into the car because they had to go to the train station. He reluctantly did it.

Roni took her son off the hood of the car and put his car seat into the carrier base in the backseat next to her father. She didn't want her son so close to her father right at that moment but she had no other choice. She was just glad that her child was encased in plastic, that her father was not quite conscious, and that she'd be picking up her husband's friend in a minute. She might not remember exactly how he and Brandon met but she knew he was a big guy trained for mortal combat.

Knowing that helped her breathe.

She got into the driver's seat and adjusted her mirrors. Her father only momentarily met her gaze in the rearview mirror before he tilted his head back and put his hands on his forehead.

Roni said nothing.

She put the key in the ignition and turned it.

Nothing happened.

The car wouldn't start: the battery had run down with the dome light shining all night.

She texted her mom to ask if she could go get her husband's friend at the train station. Her mom immediately responded to say she couldn't because she was almost at work already and plus she didn't understand why her daughter was always so unfeeling about everything that happened and never cared what her mother was going through. Roni should really not give her any more stress right when she was so emotional after the events of the previous evening, and even if

she might have maybe considered doing a favor
for Roni, even if she were perhaps available for
another twenty minutes, she wouldn't do anything
right then because she was so mad at Roni for not
even responding to her explanation in the other
text.

Roni deleted the text message from her
mother and got her son and his carrier out of the
car. She left her dad rolling around in the backseat
and walked to the house next door. She wished
she had grabbed the diaper bag or at least a
blanket. She wanted to be more prepared. But it
was too late. She rang the doorbell.

Her neighbor answered. Roni extended
her son's carrier and said, "Can I borrow your car
for a half-hour? I'll fill up the tank." Her neighbor
didn't say a word. She reached for the baby
carrier, dug into a pocket, and handed Roni her
keys.

BLEACH & WHITE TOWELS

After work—fuck that bullshit job—I get home and give in. Sometimes I can't get back up off the couch all night. It's not any one thing. I just don't know what duties matter, what obligations I care about, or how much to let myself be exploited by these assholes who think one person can do six peoples' jobs. American dream. Are you freaking kidding me? Who the hell makes it happen? I don't see how it's possible. A house? Marriage? Kids?

I'm tapping the base of the entertainment center with my shoe and slouch down. My neck's bent against the back of the couch and my butt's hanging off the cushions. I'm glad I don't have a girlfriend. Dating's too expensive. One dinner and a movie and I can hardly pay my rent.

There's not crap on TV anymore. I throw a frozen French bread pizza in the toaster oven, go back to the couch, grab the remote, flip around for a while, watch some news, maybe a little SportsCenter, but what's the point?

The Brewers suck right now. They'll never amount to anything with Davey Lopes.

The timer reminds me to get up. By no stretch of the imagination is this pathetic pizza a supreme. There is one shaving of sausage and a layer of cheese I can see through on top of the thin slab of bread. Flakes of red and green pepper placed at statistically optimal distances from one another seem to repel the tiny cubes of pepperoni that dot the top.

Still. They don't cut corners on packaging. Some dude stares up at me from the pizza box in the trash. He's supposed to be a fighter pilot, an ideal. His red scarf is blowing back in the wind. His eyes are cast to the heavens beyond. Dashing.

Dude's got a fucking mustache and a tousled animated haircut. He's wearing goggles on his head. And his stylized WWII garb would still get more women than I ever could.

I look at the clock. It's almost eight. Whether or not I show up, Judson's always got a shot of Tullamore Dew sitting in a glass on the bar for me at eight o'clock. To have a drink waiting for you at the bar when you get there is a great sign of significance.

I don't really care that much.

But I usually go. Some people put on a new shirt to go out at night. I never do. I've never really understood it. I just go in my work clothes. The bar on the corner is brick, has a cracked set of curved cement steps that no one's ever gonna fix, and has too many neon signs for the size of the windows. There are two small Harleys parked on the sidewalk. Who the hell parks on the sidewalk?

I open the door and camel bells slap the back side. A few other regular patrons look up from listening to the bartender read out loud. He does that sometimes. Seems to get a kick out of it on slow nights. He holds a book and says, "And I am dirty with its satisfaction." I rattle the door, like applause maybe, like I'm sort of making fun of him, too. Nothing crazy. Nothing out of control. Just enough to bring him down a peg. The camel bells smack the wall once and Judson shuts the book. He doesn't look pissed and sure enough, my drink's waiting in front of my seat at the short end of the bar.

He looks me in the eye, "'And I am dirty with its satisfaction.' Isn't that great? So much in it. All the guilt. All the pleasure. All the social constructs and guises and norms and repression. I love it."

I drink slowly. "I'll love it when you get off the literary kick."

"Just waiting for Monday Night Football so the library card can go back in the closet. I can't stand baseball. Won't have it in this bar."

The Brewers suck anyway. "You got anything to eat back there?"

He starts to dig through a little fridge and produces half an egg salad sandwich, three jalapeno-pickled green beans that go in the Bloody Marys, and a fistful of pretzels stale from the humidity. He plops everything onto a paper plate that bends with the weight and shoves it over to me. "A little gold, frankincense, and myrrh for you, right there. How's that?"

Better than that crappy pizza. "I'm dirty with its satisfaction."

He turns his back, picks up a bucket, and heads for the ice maker. I watch him digging down into the chest of fused ice cubes. What the fuck is he using? Some kind of red plastic thing. "Is that a sand shovel for kids at the beach?"

"Yeah. It is."

I don't want to ask. But. I can't let it go. "Why the fuck are you using a sand shovel?"

"I don't know. I bought it last week. Thought it'd work pretty good. I hate those stainless steel scoops. The handles get too cold. And I don't like cutting ketchup jugs to make scoops either. Too much trouble. They bend and crack. This is sturdy."

"But it's a kid's toy."

"So?"

There are two women playing pool. They don't talk too much but enjoy the game. One wears black leather pants. The other's in a black leather vest. They must account for the two Harleys outside. Nebraska plates. Nice bikes. But I don't know too much about bikes. I look at the woman in the vest a little too long. She smiles. She cocks her hips. She leans on the pool cue. She opens her mouth and touches her tongue to the tapering length of the wood.

Jesus. Who wants to deal with all that? I've gotta work in the morning. I swivel on my stool, put both elbows on the bar, and watch Judson dump ice over the beers. "Those girls in for Summerfest, you think? I'm not going this year. Too many people. Too much traffic."

"It's Harley's 100th though too. That could be it. Or just traveling."

"The 100th was last year."

"Right." I can't eat egg salad sandwiches. Shit's nasty. "How's their game?"

"Better than yours. What do you think about my egg salad? Never made it before, but I had a craving."

"Not bad. Needs to be on toast though."

"Toast? I've never had egg salad on toast. I'll try it."

He gets summoned to the other end of the bar. I pick up a paper and suck on a green bean. I flip slowly through the Journal Sentinel. After a while Judson wanders back and starts washing glasses.

I hold up the paper, turn an article toward him so he can see the headline and photo. "Did you see this about Kenny Chesney and Uncle Kracker on Saturday? Bizarre."

"Yeah, the lineup's fucked this year. I used to know more of the smaller bands. Now I barely care."

We're silent for a little while. It gets later. More people start coming in. They fill up the bar around me and the bartender gets busy. I read an article about zoning regulations. I read another article about various parking tribulations for Summerfest. I read part two in a three-part series about the zebra mussel infestation in the Great Lakes and its damaging effects on the ecosystem. I say to Judson, "Have you ever heard of an invasive species?" But he doesn't answer. I keep reading. The mussels come from the Caspian Sea and other foreign ballast waters of oceangoing ships that come to port in Chicago, Detroit, and Green Bay. They make a hell of a mess of pipes apparently. I drink the High Life. The wet bottle makes rings on the newspaper. The bikers settle up and get on their way to wherever.

I move a coaster with two fingers like it's part of an air hockey game. I say to Judson, "Whatever happened with Lacy?"

He rubs the back of his hand across his nose.

I'm hitting the coaster against the bottom of my beer bottle wondering if he's going to respond when he says, "She decided to keep it."

I look back at the red sand shovel left in the ice maker. "You gonna marry her?"

"Who? Lacy? Fuck no. I'm not marrying Lacy. Why would I want to deal with her shit for the rest of my life?"

"So what're you gonna do?"

"Get a fucking lawyer, I guess."

An hour goes by. Judson cuts the air conditioning and has me open up the windows since he's busy mixing mojitos for some out-of-towners who had heard of them on "Sex and the City." They probably aren't great mojitos, but the girls seemed content to pretend. "They're dirty with the satisfaction," he mouths to me while the girls giggle together.

I tilt my head back and smile in recognition.

"When you get a chance, bring me a little more of this High Life, and those green beans. They're great."

He comes back my way, "I know. I grow the beans in an empty lot next to my house then I pickle them here. I use white wine vinegar, onion, garlic, about ten red chilies, some jalapenos, rock salt, and pickling spice. Boil it up. Two weeks in the cellar and they're ready. My grandma used to make a pickle similar to it with all sorts of vegetables but not quite as hot. But I love these with a vodka or Bloody Mary. Nice offset for the flavors."

"You should sell them to all these type of fucks, folks you know. They'd give you a fortune for 'em."

"Not my style. I like the Ball Mason jars. The lids especially. And I like the quiet morning making them couple times a year. I want a tradition, not another job out of it."

Someone puts some money in the old juke box. Jimmy Cliff. Outside, a couple of guys tie a German shepherd to the stop sign and come in for a game of darts. I drink two more beers and watch the dog from the window as the evening moves on. The dog turns his head watching people walk by on the sidewalk. Then he settles down and falls asleep.

Conan has Emilio Estevez on as a guest. The TV's muted so I have no idea what brought Emilio onto a talk show. But his chat washes by with the rest of it.

Then it is just me and Judson.

He says, "You think I'll be a good dad?"

"You know you're gonna be better than mine."

He laughs.

I get off the stool, put the chairs up on the tables, shut the windows, turn off the neon signs, and check the bathrooms for anything vile while Judson cleans up the bar. He lays the stainless steel tools out on a clean towel to dry.

He sets a shot up on the bar, "For your troubles, man. Thanks."

I drink the shot. "No trouble."

He wipes the bar down. He wipes the tables down, wipes the metal work down, tosses the old white towels into the little stainless steel bar sink, fills the sink with cold water, and adds a splash of bleach. He swirls the towels and rinses his hands. "They'll sit overnight. You ready?"

FOR THE MAN WHO BOUGHT ME COFFEE AND WAS SHOT IN THE HEAD SOON AFTER

I have seen your
smile often tonight
lying on the freezer floor.

Did you know it would
happen when you pulled
up a chair and called me
beautiful?

Did you put a prayer
in my little white cup?

Were you talking to strangers
(Funny to think me strange)
to avoid your thoughts?
You knew they were
coming, didn't you?
But you didn't know when.
So much like the rest of us
but sooner.

Was I safe to you
or did I look naive and happy?
Were you just glad someone would
go on?

And the thought of you—
who flattered me with no reserve,
wanted absolutely nothing,
and felt so good—
kneeling down with a couple of
friends in the freezer
(One on either side, I'll bet)
hands tied behind your back

looking at the door.
Hoping someone would come for you.
Wishing they hadn't.

And why did they come?
I suppose it's rude to ask.

Scared. Were you scared?
How long did you kneel there
with their words over you?
I'm glad it was cold.
I hope you were numb for your
execution.
I certainly hope you were.

I don't know why I didn't hear you
cry out. Voice submerged
by always-on-top-flattery,
beautiful faces, French,
and laughing cigarettes.

But I do remember your leaning
closer than I might have expected.

and I do remember your looking into

my eyes, hiding something

precious in me.

Anyway,

Thank you for the coffee

and for stabbing your smile

deep enough.

HOLLACE AND SOME GIRL

Black shoes need shining at the airport and grab a newspaper too. Hollace Dupree sat behind his paper not so much reading it as thanking it for dividing him from the throngs of travelers and from the shoeshiner. At page fourteen, he thought slowly whether he should have a glass of orange juice or a nice cup of coffee before his flight. Both would cost way too much, but he was above taking a thermos to the airport and actually hadn't thought of that until just now. He hated flying coach. The complimentary beverages on the plane could not be trusted unless carbonated. Airplane coffee was mealy and the orange juice often had a metallic taste or worse, had to be consumed from a miniscule plastic tub.

After nodding, smiling, and tipping the burly shoeshiner in a grand act of escape, Mr. Dupree strode across the wide corridor breaking through streams of early-morning travelers without much notice to family integrity, shopping bags bearing the visages of cartoon characters, or the momentum of gaggles of flight attendants with their wheeled carry-ons. All the various looks of disgust were lost on Hollace Dupree who moved through life from one destination to another head down and inattentive to others. Coffee. Small. Black. Thank you.

Once seated on the plane after a suitable wait at the gate and the usual boarding of the vessel by rows starting from the rear, Hollace Dupree watched the airport staff from his window without interest. He kept an eye on the conveyor belt half hoping to catch sight of his own bags being loaded onto the plane. He was uneasy and thought that if his bags were on the plane then he was certainly going to the right place.

As interesting as the search for his luggage was, it was the men who were working under the plane that eventually held his attention. The gloves and the uniforms and the grease were all such glorious accessories to the fuel lines, baggage carts, meal trucks, and so on which were teeming around the huge jet. A man holding fluorescent flashlights stood back from the crowd adjusting his knee pads. His brown curls set themselves free of a cap and then disappeared again, sweating. As the jet engines began to roar several of the workers, pulling off gloves and turning their faces toward the cold morning sun, laughed together over something easily understood while wearing ear protection.

Upon witnessing their laughter Hollace felt himself the intruder. He looked away quickly not having meant any harm. He concentrated instead on the crease in his pants, pinching it together at various points and assuring its crisp respectability. Then he turned to the safety card for a minute and focused thoughts about a water landing. It seemed an impossibility that his seat could in any way become a flotation device. Some child had left a drawing in the seat pocket. It was a bawdy array of ogres and what might have passed for either a princess or a rather sick-making pile of fruit. Hollace reviewed the sheet from several perspectives and replaced it gingerly behind the on-board catalog. He ran his finger across the bendable wire that would close the bag which Mr. Dupree had always thought suited popcorn more than human emesis. His eyes avoided the window. But he decided that once the plane was on the runway it would be okay to watch during takeoff. For now he just waited.

It was a business flight in 1999. Virtually every passenger had some combination of the following items: power suit, laptop computer, Wall Street Journal, important-looking data sheets, stapled piles of something or other to review, and coffee. Hollace Dupree was not an exception. Hollace Dupree was never an exception. He wore a gray suit and a white shirt.

His tie was interesting but conservative and most likely was purchased in a department store. He had not traveled beyond what his business required, and this morning he was returning home from somewhere else. He did not have gifts to take home for anyone and would not consider finding anyone for whom to take gifts home. Hollace unknowingly defined himself through his career. He attended charity functions with clients, played golf and tennis with clients, went to an Episcopal church to meet new clients, and sent sympathy cards when his clients passed away. He was an accountant.

Without another thing to look at in order to pass the time, Hollace wondered whether it were worth soliciting some amenity from the airline woman who was near enough to be asked. But as he tried to decide between creamer which he didn't need for the coffee or a pillow which would take up too much of his tiny allotment of space, the flight attendant's attention was drawn toward the front of the plane.

Hollace looked to see what could possibly have preempted his needs.

Never had he witnessed such an abomination. There, on the rubber mat outside the cockpit, stood a girl. Not so unremarkable even on a 6:07 a.m. business flight, but this girl was wearing a hot pink gown with hoop skirts.

The skirt must have been made with at least fifteen yards of material and there was bulk and fluff added by several layers of crinolines and other undergarments. The skirt was accompanied by an extremely tight bodice. There were times when women had ribs removed to fit themselves into such bodices, and one wondered whether this girl had required such an operation. Several vertical shafts seemed to run through the bodice. And a panel of white muslin was brought together in an even more restraining manner by a network of ribbons. The supposed concept of this invention was that it allowed her bosom to sit so precariously that it might at any time happen to fall into plain view.

She boarded the plane at 6:05 a.m. in a fit of rage. Her arms were flying around her, at one moment wiping away tears, at another tugging at the skirt that would not fit into the aisle. And those same arms seemed to reflect utter despair which required much attention. She snapped at the flight attendant. "What—? Do you have a problem? You could help me, you know, you and your polyester-perfect polka dot bow tie. What is up with that bow tie? How do you get that ridiculous ribbon so tangled around your neck and make it look intentional? Huh? And that manicure too. Red. You have all those same red nails. Do you think I want to stare at your red nails and your gold rings and your hair-sprayed French twists when I'm flying to Toronto? Do you?"

This was long enough before 9/11 that members of the flight crew had not fully relinquished their servile roles in favor of a more enforceable intimidation. And too bad, really; much might have been different. But as it was, the flight attendant ran her tongue over her teeth and swallowed twice before she replied in a pleasant but firmly kind voice, "I'm afraid we are not destined for Toronto this morning, ma'am. Do you require assistance finding another gate? We would like to push back as soon as possible."

The girl dropped her arms to her sides and stared into the flight attendant with black eyes. "There are a thousand small trolls like you rushing into life this morning in high heels. And do you know what? Color contacts are made with the rotting placentas of rabbits."

The flight attendant receded somehow, coughing back tears with her hand unconsciously patting her upswept hair.

The woman in the pink dress succumbed to the rage and began a public fit of sobbing tears.

"My lord." Hollace whispered to himself with incredulity, awe, and embarrassment.

The girl was a disgrace. Her hair was disheveled but looked a recent bouncing mane of banana curls. She wore gloves and lace and ribbons and bows. Gaudy pewter and glass jewelry seemed an awful burden but sporadically flashed rainbows around the cabin as she thrashed against the lavatory door. On top of all this she was wearing a dark green backpack covered with embroidery, strange patches, and small activist pins. But the ensign of her absolute displacement from the nineteenth century was that she had a tattoo of small roses that wrapped around her biceps. She kept sobbing with such overt pain that women found themselves disgusted by the trails of her mascara, and men watched her heaving chest with high hopes.

Several minutes passed. No one wanted to take control of the situation. The flight attendants certainly would not and the pilots did their best to busy themselves with knobs and gauges. The other passengers furtively looked past their papers hoping to catch a quip or anecdote from the girl. Each was planning a witty icebreaker to explain his or her late arrival. An apple-cheeked maniac escaping the throes of antebellum society and flinging obscenities is certainly a better story than the usual broken fuel lines and fog delays.

Finally realizing that the aisle could not possibly be negotiated in all her finery, the girl began to tug wildly at the skirts. And she left behind her a pile of crinoline, hot pink taffeta, and at least three bone hoops which the flight attendant nearest to her heaped into a storage bin generally reserved for strollers.

The girl stood in bloomers looking for a seat. She scratched her leg with the opposite foot. She was wearing black stockings and black boots with laces that crisscrossed themselves halfway up to her knee. There were uncomfortable laughs, shakes of voyeurs' papers, and the *tsk*s and gasps which are often heard at such times.

Hollace, choosing the lesser of two evils, allowed his eyes to go back to the men outside. He took his chances that they might notice his vicariously enjoying their fun.

The girl, still crying uncontrollably, flung herself toward the empty seat in the 14th row. As if to assure the other passengers that she had a right to be there, she sat down next to Hollace Dupree with a deliberate flounce, settled herself, and after kicking him more than once she was established there and cried freely. She leaned against the seat in front of her sobbing breathlessly.

Hollace sat braced in his seat. Every muscle in his body was tense with her proximity. Though he was concerned for her happiness he was also concerned with his own, and he could smell her. From the corner of his eye he could see the line of pale flesh that ran from her elbow along the curve of her armpit and up over her breast as she sat with her arms folded on top of the seat in front of her. He could also sense her thighs through the thin wrinkles of the muslin bloomers. Just as she could not stop crying to breathe, Hollace Dupree could not possibly lift the weight of restraint from his own breast in order to catch some air.

He swallowed hard several times and felt his Adam's apple against the tight collar. He pursed his lips and relaxed them again. He tilted his head, up and back, up and back, all the while looking out the window. The back of his neck was

119

hot, surely a result of air not circulating well through the synthetic materials from which airplane headrests tend to be made. His eyebrows danced between wide-eyed inspection and fervent disapproval. And although so much motion was occurring above his shoulders, from the neck down he was clenched. His left hand held his pants so tightly that the carefully-placed crease was dying by strangulation under his grip.

Around them the passengers still regarded the girl with some fear. Not because she looked abnormal, but because the entire plane echoed with her dramatic crying. By this time she was beating the seat in front of her with a small fist and screaming, "No. You fucking jackass bastard! No. God damn it. No!" Over and over and over again. And wailing through her tears in such a way that the flight attendants retreated to the ends of the cabin in two closely-huddled groups and unconsciously spun their heavy wedding bands around bony red-nailed fingers. One of the women went into the restroom, took off her bow tie, and retied it altogether. Those passengers who were sitting nearby became such a shifting mass of energy that static electricity built as frictive pantyhose and wool pants rubbed against fireproof synthetic seats.

The copilot quickly slammed the door that divided the flight crew from the cabin. Even though there were no reassuring or informative announcements, the plane started and the pilots began to recover the few lost minutes. The plane shifted with anticipation and began to roll out of the gate, but there was no sign that the girl would ever stop crying. It was apparent all other parties were diligently avoiding the situation, which left Hollace Dupree alone to comfort the poor thing, although it was hard to feel sorry for someone so violent.

Drawing in a quick breath to sustain his determination he prioritized his possible courses of action. At the office he might offer her a cup of coffee, water, or even juice. He could allow her to sit at his desk for a few minutes to quiet herself. However, they were not at the office. He considered the situation. There seemed so few resources. He might offer her the window seat, but that seemed excessive. He decided instead upon, "Hello there. Hmm. Let's see. Here's my card."

Now, this might not have been the most tactful thing to say, but Hollace Dupree was practiced at the statement and knew he could rely on it for a response. He wasn't sure his sentimental skills would project confidence. The girl, it seemed at first, reacted positively. In one motion she cast the backpack onto the floor in the aisle, ran her sweaty hands over her face several times, threw herself against her own seat back, and grabbed the card.

Rendon and Associates Inc.

Hollace Dupree, CPA

Outstanding Balance and Property

Humbly serving the community since 1964

Having read the card and with the stultifying shock of its presentation wearing off, the girl replied, "Don't you want to know why I'm in such a fucking fit? Why do you people always think about business? I mean for God's sake I need some humanity here. Look at me. Do you think I'm going to need a—." She looked at the card for some evidence of his position. "Whatever you are? I'm a complete wreck, and all you can think of is how you can score one for your business? I hate you."

Hollace decided that while he probably should have offered her the window seat initially, he certainly would not do so now. This girl was a defiant creature. "Always thinking about scoring and business." The thought! What he would do for any other seat on that plane. His character did not allow him to make such a request now. But this was too much.

The girl continued her attack. "What are you anyway? Going off to some rich business brunch. Going to look at some expensive graphs and eat catered food off of paper plates. Or are you going to go back to your wife after a night of fucking your whore in another city? Don't forget to put your wedding ring back on, asshole."

"I am not married." Hollace drew his handkerchief out of his pocket and patted his face. Though the cabin was cool he seemed to be sweating.

"Oh, I get it. So you like it from the boys down in the mailroom. I should have known. Fucking handmade pointy shoes. You're wearing purple socks, for Christ's sake."

The socks along with the tie which Hollace was wearing had been a present from his sister-in-law the previous Christmas. In any event he knew that neither was purple; they were, in fact, plum. His sister-in-law had assured him they were not purple. Hollace Dupree would never wear purple socks. These were definitely plum. The plane was just completing its ascent. Hollace had completely missed takeoff. He was incensed.

Sitting up straighter and turning toward the girl he asked, "Is there anything that I might do to protect myself against this early-morning tirade?"

The girl was taken aback. She looked around for her defense. No one supported her. The other passengers were busy with their papers and coffee, listening. "You know why I'm on this plane? Because this is the gate where my friend was working. She works at the counter for this airline, and she gave me a boarding pass. We go out all the time and she always says that if I want to go somewhere I should just come to the counter where she works and she'll slip me on the plane. So here I am. I don't know where this plane is even going. And you know what? I don't have to, because I don't care."

Hollace decided from this obvious display of insecurity that the girl was probably around twenty-three years of age—old enough to have serious problems but still too young to handle them by herself. He was regaining strength.

She adjusted her bodice.

Hollace watched her writhing long enough to decide that she must be exceedingly uncomfortable. Then, without daring to try, he wished he had looked a little longer.

As though she had come full circle by that statement, she returned to his question. "Yes. You can. If you want me to shut up you can tell me why all men are such assholes."

Maybe only twenty-one judging from the overwhelming generalization. "Do you mean any particular man, because I certainly cannot speak for us all?" Hollace tried not to smile at the girl. He wanted her to be assured that he was taking her plight seriously.

She saw the kindness in his eyes. "Okay, well then, Jake. Tell me why Jake is such an asshole."

"Jake of Jake's Lawn Care or Jake of Jake's Pizza?"

A beautiful young pink smile. "Jake of my asshole ex-boyfriend cheating ass, Jake."

"Oh. Not an entrepreneur of the usual sort, I see."

"More usual than you think, Mr. —," again consulting the business card, "Dupree."

"I suppose this is so."

"You never cheated on a girlfriend?"

Hollace considered the question. After dismissing a confusing incident in college that may have fit the definition of infidelity but certainly was a misunderstanding by all parties, he decided to go with his statistical average which was a decided, "No."

"Why not?"

Oh. These questions. Why not look out over the billow of cloud that spread out to the horizon making the view from the window a treasure for a moment? It was only six in the morning. Why not look at the sunrise? What a rare thing to be so close to it. Why think about some foolish young man 30,000 feet below and miles behind? He avoided the question since she was obviously torturing herself. Self-inflicted romance problems are prominent at nineteen— but she must be older than that.

"I never cheated on a girlfriend because I never considered the stuff of romance to be a game. One might cheat at cards and board games, not in relationships. Relationships are business. Negotiation and respect. Always took it as serious business, I'm afraid. May I ask a question of you, Miss—?" He solicited her last name.

"Well, as of one thirty this morning it's Mrs. Jake Russell. We eloped."

Definitely twenty-two. "Well, Mrs. Russell—"

"Don't call me that. He's such a rat bastard."

"Regardless of your name then, why did you board the plane this morning in such antiquated attire?"

She tore at the dress's narrow cap shoulders. She pulled off some cheap earrings and wiped her nose in a disgusting manner with the back of her hand. "I fucking hate my job. Do you know that I have four of these dresses? And on the Fourth of July I have to wear one that is all red, white, and blue, with stars and a fucking patriotic parasol. Eight years. First I sold lemonade. That wasn't so bad. I smoked cigarettes with all the Mexicans and only had to wear some stupid paper pioneer hat. I work at Merton Village and Historic Theme Park. It's awful.

"Now I'm the folly girl in the cafe where they serve cotton candy and popcorn to a bunch of little kids. Jake is a blacksmith. He makes all

sorts of stupid trinkets out of old nails and sells
them all for about seventy-five times what they're
worth. So after work yesterday we went out like
we always do—two and a half years. He told me
to meet him by the blacksmith shop and we rode
his motorcycle over to the water and got married
by a gambling boat captain. Nice wedding. Can
you believe I stayed with that dick for two and a
half years?"

Her vulgar language was beginning to
wear on Hollace. He winced.

"Sorry. Are you like my mom's age or
what?"

Hoping he was much younger than the
mother and closer in fact to the age of the girl,
Hollace hedged, "Well, how old is your mother?"

"I don't know. I never met her. It's just a
figure of speech, you know."

Hollace didn't know. He had no idea in
fact. "Yes. I suppose so."

The flight attendant appeared with the
beverage cart. Hollace asked politely about the
brand of orange juice and requested a ginger ale as

well, if it weren't too much trouble. The girl ordered a Bloody Mary with four extra shots of vodka. Hollace noticed that the stewardess ignored the alcohol limit. Everyone on the plane was indebted to Hollace for dealing with the girl. There was a look of thanksgiving. Noting this and in a fit of generosity Hollace whipped out his wallet and paid for the girl's drinks.

"You didn't need to do that." She pulled at the plastic on the lid of the vodka with her teeth. Once she had ripped the cellophane and spit it onto the floor she dumped half the vodka into her drink and drank the rest straight.

He watched her with a combination of sickness and intrigue. "It is your wedding day. It's the least I can do." It is true that Hollace was interested in hearing the rest of this story. "So who is the harlot?"

"The what?"

"Jake's other—well, the other woman."

"Oh, the cheap-ass whore?"

"Having never met her, I'll reserve my judgment. But for the purposes of discussion and

clarity, yes, the— well, the cheap-ass whore."
Hollace was proud of himself. And smiled with
closed lips.

They both laughed and toasted each
other. Hollace was careful not to spill his half-
filled glass, and her drink sloshing wildly ran over
onto the back of her hand. She sucked the liquid
quickly and licked her entire hand clean. Hollace
thought this was obscene and found himself
intently tapping his index finger on the tray. He
finished his drink and slowly poured another
small amount of juice into his glass.

After opening a packet of peanuts and
swallowing the entire contents without really
chewing, the girl went on. "Well. God knows
what her name is. People call her Bitsy. Isn't that
disgusting? She's no one. She takes tickets at the
Scrambler. Big hair. Bad jeans. You've seen a
thousand like her at places like that. Real skinny,
you know?"

Hollace adjusted the vent above his head
so that more air was flowing over him. "I guess

I'm not a big fan of amusement parks. Wouldn't know the type most likely, I'm afraid."

The girl nodded. "Right. She's trash, if you want to know the truth." Without asking permission the girl poured one of the tiny vodka bottles into Hollace's cup. "Have a screwdriver, Hollace Dupree. You need it after listening to all this crap. Besides you paid for it."

He did not refuse. He probably couldn't have.

There was a lull in their conversation through a bit of turbulence. They kept drinking for a few quiet minutes. Hollace looked out over the white cloud bank that undulated under them and reflected sunlight everywhere. He thought of Jake somewhere down there. Just married and wondering where his wife was on an overcast day. What a glorious morning. What an odd beginning. The girl rummaged through her backpack for something.

Thrusting some worn paper and a strip of photos from a picture booth the girl, like a television lawyer, burst out, "See. Look at this shit. After we got married he wanted to take me to a hotel but I was cold so he let me wear his jacket on the bike. These were in the pocket. I jumped off the bike when he was going almost twenty miles an hour. I grabbed a bottle of Jack from a shitty little convenience mart and just got a cab right to the airport."

Hollace looked at the pictures. They verged on pornographic. He wondered why this girl married such a rather ugly young man. She was very pretty and judging from these photographs he was not at all up to her standard. His mind wandered as he stared blankly at the pictures. How could she possibly ride a motorcycle in that bizarre dress? Resolutely he informed her, "You could do much better than this boy. I suggest getting an annulment."

"A what?"

"An annulment. Void your marriage. Have it taken away. Erased."

"But I love him."

Hollace said nothing. He held the strip of pictures up for her to see.

Tears formed in her eyes and she took the liberty of ripping Hollace's breast pocket handkerchief from his suit and blowing her nose in it. "It's so cheap to just quit. I want to work it out. What if that didn't mean anything to him? He loves me, you know."

Not quite believing her, Hollace refrained from pointing out that running from the situation might not be how to work it out. "Some things are not worth fighting for. Sometimes, on days like this, one must simply assess the situation and resolve to walk away. Simply let the oppressive nature of the situation be what it is and submit to it." Hollace finished his drink resolutely. "Then, and it will no doubt be in short order, you will rise above the thing to new heights. And you will be the better for it."

"You're one of those people that think every bad experience just builds character and crap like that, huh?"

"Possibly." He did not like feeling cornered.

"I'm more of the 'shit happens' school myself."

Nodding repeatedly in a mildly drunken state, Hollace showed his understanding.

"Or maybe I should just go balls out and fuck somebody raw. Don't you think? Then we'd be even. Then we could just go on." She recanted when she saw he was shocked. "Annulment. Yeah. I guess. How do you get it?"

Hollace explained what little he knew and gave the names of service offices that should certainly be able to give her assistance. He was a resourceful man.

They bought two more drinks and talked about her options as the plane burned off fuel, got lighter, made its step climb to higher altitudes.

"But it's so embarrassing. God. It's so embarrassing."

Hollace pointed out that throwing tantrums in hoop skirts on an airplane might be in a similar vein. The girl, obviously drunk, laughed. They laughed together about their first impressions of each other. Hollace explained how thoroughly she had drawn the attention of every other passenger. The girl was uplifted by the story and pleased that people had been paying attention to her. She swore she had been unaware. Maybe twenty-four. The girl apologized for making fun of his purple socks. They most certainly were plum. And besides, she liked them.

The girl decided to change into something more normal so her sister wouldn't freak out when she met her at the gate. The plane began its descent.

He complimented her tattoo. They talked easily as she unlaced her boots. He commented on the dexterity she had with the laces and she reminded him how long she had been wearing them. She showed him the blisters the boots caused and he noticed the silver ring on her second toe. It had been a gift from a friend. It was from Athens. The friend went to Greece every year with her grandmother to visit her great aunt. Hollace listened and stared at the toes that she wiggled over his lap. Ten toes with rosy gold polish.

She stood up in the aisle organizing her bag and digging to the bottom for a pair of jeans. She leaned over the bag. Hollace watched her. Her springy curled hair danced around her shoulders. Sitting against the seat had caused them to become ridden with static electricity and more tangled. Hollace imagined this might be what she should have looked like anyway, waking up after her wedding night. He looked at the way her neck stopped and spilled out over the collar bone and ran into two simple reservoirs, her breasts, caught in the cups of that strange 19th century bodice. Without thinking he reached out and ran his finger from her chin down over them. She jerked her head up. They stared at one another.

"So beautiful." His lower lip was caught by his teeth.

The girl grabbed her clothes and went to the bathroom to change.

Hollace was unsure what had just happened. He did not meet the gaze of the older woman across the aisle and instead turned his face to the window, to the back of the seat in front of him, to the tray-table's latch, then into the seat next to him where the girl's backpack sat agape. A bra hung out from the bag. Hollace put the bra into the bag, touching it with deference, and looked out the window. He felt the pressure change in his ears. They were going down quickly.

When she returned the girl sat straight in the chair, seat belt fastened, legs crossed away from him, flipping through the onboard catalog without seeing the merchandise. Hollace wished there was something he could say. His fingers ran up and down along the crease of his pants. He pursed his lips repeatedly and tried to breathe against the constraints of his collar around his Adam's apple. The plane landed with a mild jolt.

Nothing was said.

Still seated, the girl was ready with her backpack on as they taxied to the gate. Hollace waited to retrieve his briefcase from under the seat. He did not wish to disturb her again. After waiting for the door to open the girl pushed her way to the front of the plane to retrieve her skirts.

Hollace sighed and picked up his dirty rumpled handkerchief from her seat where it had been left, used and forgotten. He hoped she would not notice as he passed behind her at the front of the cabin.

But she saw him coming. A flight attendant was trying to make sense of the hoops and billows of material. Thankful momentarily, the girl smiled at Hollace as she gathered her skirts from the flight attendant's arms. "Well, be off to your exploits then. And hand out a thousand of your Outstanding Balance business cards."

Allowing the bustling business people to rush past them Hollace looked at his clean black shoes. Then he cleared his throat and directed his attention toward her. "Actually no. I am afraid you will be the last to receive one. I was fired over the phone at five-thirty this morning." He put his culprit hand in his pocket and cleared his throat. "I found an error somewhere in excess of a quarter million dollars on the company books recently. Apparently the higher-ups did not appreciate my accuracy. Or perhaps having fully realized the error, they needed to downsize in order to cut costs." And he was past her, moving up the corridor with dignity. "Good luck to you, though."

The girl stood tangled in pink taffeta wishing and unwishing. She dumped the taffeta in the gate entrance and called after him, "Hollace!" He was already quite far ahead and she had to call many times. But he returned earnestly and granted her request to wait in the bar while she made a phone call. In fact made two.

"Hey, Larise. Yeah, I told Mom last night … Of course she freaked. She gave me the whole why-can't-you-be-like-your-big-sister talk and then started crying and all that routine … Yeah, I'm happy. Happy enough. I just didn't want to bother with putting together all the invitations and shit … I know … The boat thing wasn't what I had in mind either … Well, you can come out in June. We're going to have a reception and everything then when his uncle's family visits."

She looked toward Hollace. Travelers streamed through the corridor reading gate information, hugging, hurrying, showing their children the planes and the big windows, and talking. There were everyone: Indians and Blacks and Asians and Hispanics and Whites and Old People on Carts and Hollace waited for her in the bar as though he might never leave. There was nothing on the table and he seemed to be unaware of all those drinking around him. Instead his head was cocked slightly and he stared contentedly at an elevated television.

The phone conversation went on, "No, don't worry about it. That was a stupid idea. I'm at the hotel. He's asleep. I just wanted to call and tell you that I'm not really crazy enough to leave him. I just got pissed off when I found those pictures. But he said it didn't mean anything. Kind of a last fling before we got married I guess… Yeah, I'll call you in a few days." And then she called Jake. "I know. I know. I'm sorry. Don't cry. I'm coming home tonight and everything's going to be great. Okay? I love you, too."

She smiled as she hung up the phone. Hollace watched her pulling her wedding ring off and shoving it into the pocket of her jeans and wondered for a moment what he was getting into, but he didn't really care. He picked up her backpack and carried it on his shoulder. It looked odd next to his conservative suit. With his briefcase in the other hand, he walked upright and gray. She danced around him with curving hips and bright raggedy clothes. He paid for the taxi. She nudged him in the ribs. She rearranged his hair. She said careful things that allowed him to laugh, and easy vengeance was her consummation.

ANGELS ON HORSEBACK

Kitchens breathe easily in big families. There is a blur of aunts and uncles leaning on counters. Teenage cousins avoid obligation in the basement surfacing only to refill a bowl of tortilla chips. Little nephews play with string cheese on the floor. At the end of the kitchen there is an island where neighbors are sitting on bar stools drinking mai tais, white wine, and sangria. They get up to take turns throwing a doll's head (a beloved dog toy) into the living room. Charlie, the golden retriever, bounds back to the slow-swirling group and looks around among different friendly faces before choosing one and offering up his drool-covered prize.

A twenty-six-year-old woman, the new wife of one of the older grandchildren, stands awkwardly apart from the group. The loudest neighbor demands that she come toss the doll's head. She declines but so as not to seem too standoffish she instead makes a large gesture of maturely closing the basement stairs door in an effort to improve her political position in the familial hierarchy. Who does that surly nineteen-year-old think he is to let a door stand open in the middle of the way as he rushes and rumbles down the steps?

But. Who is she to care? So she leans over and picks up the lone tortilla chip he dropped from his refilled bowl lest it get crushed and require whatever reprimand might come out with the vacuum.

Mrs. Hamel from church is carrying serving dishes out to the screened-in porch. She seems never quite pleased with the platters' spatial relations. The buffet under the kitchen window goes through different permutations. Deviled eggs, potato salad, coleslaw, orange Jell-O and carrot salad, teriyaki chicken wings, and mint-frosted chocolate chip brownies dance, leapfrog, slide around, and push back in her old, gnarled, manicured hands until she's satisfied.

No one is listening. But Mrs. Swindan answers what must have been a question posed by that new wife of one of the older grandchildren, "Angels on horseback are just baked oysters wrapped in bacon," then raises her voice to shout toward the porch, "Mrs. Hamel. How do you make your Christmas fruit salad?"

Mrs. Hamel hears the question but doesn't bother raising her voice much. She's folding napkins corner-to-corner and making a pinwheel pile. "The oranges are from Central America. None of this grocery store nonsense. Mine come directly from the grove to my back door. Lord knows what infestations I'm ushering in on the fruit, but I don't care. I'm an old lady, I like good oranges, and I hate pesticides."

When the twenty-six-year-old comes through the doorway carrying the fruit salad, Mrs. Hamel points to one of two empty places of honor, and the prized dish gets turned ninety degrees counterclockwise.

"So you cut the oranges. Lots of them. Let the juice run in too. Then the apples. I like the Galas from Washington State, but you can be more flexible with the apples. Just don't use those big red ones covered in soapy wax from the store. They're mealy and awful. Use a good baking apple over a good lunchbox apple. They won't take on as much fluid and mush down on you. I've even used the Granny Smith. They are tart but firm and get balanced by so much soft sweetness in the salad. The Golden Delicious is fine if you can't find the Gala and don't want the tart zing of the Granny Smith. But the Golden will get soft after a while."

Mrs. Swindan only asked to be polite. She drifts off from the kitchen to get the three-tiered cake plate from upstairs. But. The young woman keeps listening.

Mrs. Hamel folds more napkins. "After the apples go in, squirt it with some lemon juice to prevent all those apples from browning. The orange juice just isn't acidic enough. Then the maraschinos. Halves or quarters, whichever you have time for. Lastly, the coconut. Best to grate it fresh yourself from the meat of a coconut. But I'll admit I've only done that once. It was such a mess getting into that thing! It took a screwdriver and a hammer and a lot of words that I'd rather not employ to get that sucker open. The blessed thing rolled off my counter so many times that I ended up on the floor with it. My legs holding it steady then hacking at it with that screwdriver and hammer. Awful. And the milk got all over my shoes and dress when I finally did get it open.

"So I do recommend the store-bought, fully-processed, shredded coconut. A quarter to half a bag. A good fistful is about right. And really it works out better than the fresh coconut because the dry coconut takes up the maraschino juice and the orange juice for blended flavor. But that coconut is mainly for texture and looks. You can

leave it out if you must. It's a great salad
Christmas morning with breads and spreads.
Stollen and cream cheese every year at our
house." She smiles. "The key is high quality
oranges. A definite must. Not worth making with
crap oranges."

"Thank you, Mrs. Hamel. Someday I'll try
it out."

"Well, not until you tell me how you come
up with these beauties year after year." Mrs.
Hamel gestures toward the deviled eggs. It's clear
enough that Mrs. Hamel hates deviled eggs. But
one's recipe is never just given away. It must be
exchanged for another equally as good. And
everyone says that these particular deviled eggs
are as near to perfection as Icarus ever was to the
sun, which is much too close for Mrs. Hamel's
comfort. She slams the salt and pepper shakers
down against the table in three different places.
Nowhere seems right.

But. The young wife didn't make the
deviled eggs. So she shakes her head and points to
a tray of cookies that she only had to bake in

ready-made batches for eight to ten minutes. She says she thinks one of the neighbors made the deviled eggs and cranes her neck inside to ask. But the neighbors have their backs turned, still throwing the doll's head, and are also distracted from her uninvolved incursion by watching the middle school boys' well-matched race in a video game. So the story of the deviled eggs is never told.

Mrs. Hamel is glad not to have to listen to such rot about whoever thinks she can make the best plate of deviled eggs but also demonstrates a sort of disappointed disgust in the girl's inability to assert herself.

The young new wife of one of the older grandchildren is not just a girl and doesn't think it is her fault that the row of neighbors can't hear her asking for the deviled egg recipe. And why should she interrupt them when Mrs. Hamel doesn't even want to listen? Still, it's true enough that she isn't quite sure which one of the neighbors made them. So there is no one in particular to ask. She wanders away from Mrs.

Hamel, opens the door to the basement stairs, and disappears.

Back in the kitchen Mrs. Swindan has come downstairs. She and Mrs. Roth are working away. "Doesn't it seem unlikely?" Mrs. Swindan says it as if caught—an eagle in a tall chicken wire fence. A fight is useless. They are sisters. And so the reply from Mrs. Roth, "Mmm." She preheats the oven and begins to pour a layer of rock salt into a jelly roll pan. The sound of the salt against the metal is muffled by jazz.

The sink is full of ice. The kitchen walls bask in the last of the afternoon sun. The white wine, in glasses lined up in the window, holds glimpses of the light. Leaning on the stove, hands on the aprons, sipping periodically, the sisters clean and straighten up nothing that needs to be done. They are waiting for the oysters.

The conversation dies easily. A pattern made by a thousand arguments not bothered with in the presence of guests, like this nosy young wife of one of the older grandchildren. The matronly sisters pretend not to notice that she keeps popping up every time they both turn around. Mrs. Roth might involve her but cannot remember her name. So instead she watches a group of children trample her sugar snap peas in the garden as they squabble about who should retrieve the soccer ball. Her children and her sister's children and some children of friends are trying to be careful, but the soccer ball has wreaked havoc enough.

The peas can handle it. She turns away from the window and tries to remember the name of the young woman Mrs. Hamel must have rebuffed, picks up her glass, and puts the back of her hand against the oven door, testing the heat.

"What's Owen's new wife's name?"

"I thought you knew. She stood there hovering and I had absolutely no idea. I was about to ask."

"Mrs. Hamel must have said something to her. She slithered down the stairs two minutes ago."

"I didn't see that. Are you sure?"

"Yes. You know how she can be."

"Who?"

Mrs. Hamel overhears Mrs. Swindan and Mrs. Roth. She said, "Her name is Christa. And I didn't say a word. The girl's got no—"

But Mrs. Swindan doesn't wait for her comment. She yanks the basement door open. "Christa!"

Christa hurries up the stairs. She stands close to Mrs. Roth who quickly hands her the salad tongs. "Just toss everything together. Be sure to get the tomatoes and olives off the bottom." Mrs. Swindan doesn't bother to remind her sister that three people asked for salad without dressing and that two others hate olives, which is why things were as they were with the dressing on the bottom.

But. Mrs. Hamel forgets nothing. "What do you expect Andre to do?" Christa looks first to Mrs. Roth, who has obviously forgotten, then to Mrs. Swindan, who shakes her head, and lastly to Mrs. Hamel who throws her hands up proving herself beyond all culpability. Christa says, "I'm sorry. I didn't know."

Everyone is relieved by the sound of the garage door rising. Two men laugh heartily. One opens the door. The other backs his way up the stairs, slowly. They each hold one handle of an old metal tub. They carry it awkwardly through the door and steady it with slow steps, outstretched arms, and dictatorial statements. The women disperse like a flock of starlings that rises just a few feet and settles again on a different part of the lawn. Because they've arrived. Not the men but what they carry.

No one says a word. Everyone watches while the two men lift the tub, tilt it, slowly, slowly. One says, "Steady." And the other wraps his lips around his teeth in a grimace. "Pull it back. Yeah. Okay. Now go." They let the ocean water splash down into the sink. The oysters rattle, clatter, tumble, and fall, piling onto each other in a haze of the sea on ice.

The men tip the tub a few inches further, to be sure, to be absolutely sure. One of them grabs both handles, tips it all the way upside-down to be a hundred percent certain. Mainly for show, the other pounds the bottom of the tub.

But. Though no one expects it, one more oyster, one lodged in the crimp somehow, comes free and drops straight down onto the others.

One of the men says, "That's about twice what we had last year." Satisfied, the men retreat. The tub disappears, gets rinsed, gets forgotten again on the rafters in the garage.

The women do not hesitate to return. They talk and laugh. Their hands are deft as they wield flexible knives.

Mrs. Swindan's nine-year-old son announces, "I want to do one." The young man marries once. And his bride is Impossibility. He conquers her in time. "Let me. Let me try."

His mother hands over her knife. "Find a good one."

The boy takes the biggest oyster he sees.

His mother hands over the glove.

"I don't want to wear that."

"You have to protect your hands. It won't let you cut your fingers off."

The boy reluctantly puts on the wire mesh glove. He holds the oyster level to the ground knowing that the juice will run out if he does not. "Now what?"

"See how it's thicker down here? That's the cup. Across from that there is a sort of hinge. You want to stick the knife right into the hinge. A twist should pop it open and then you cut the bottle muscle."

"I thought it was really hard."

She smiles, knowing. "It is."

The boy, concentrating, holds the oyster with the awkward glove. He finds the hinge and struggles to get the knife tip in. The knife slips and rams into his palm but is stopped by the steel mesh of the glove. His eyes are wide.

"See; we could be on our way to the emergency room right now."

Understanding more, he tries again. He can feel it now. That place where the tip of the knife must penetrate. "I get it." He doesn't falter. The flat tip goes in. He holds the cup firmly but level in the glove and twists his knife hand enough to pop the shell open.

"Now get it loose underneath."

He cuts hesitantly. He doesn't want to lose the juice. He quits, offers up both the knife and the oyster. "I can't. You do it."

"Just keep going slowly. You'll get it."

He does not want to try. He does not want to be told to keep going. He does not want to do it wrong. He does not want to not know how. He keeps looking around, at his mother, at his father, at his aunts, at his dog, at the new wife of one of his older cousins, at his brother, who nods. The pressure of the knife is a little much and the oyster pops back, juice splashing down his wrist, lost. But the muscle was cut and he holds the oyster up so his mother will give it a squirt of lemon juice and a little Tabasco. He knows this part and sucks it down, relishing his work.

She is satisfied and grants permission for him to be dismissed. He hands back the glove and watches his mother and aunt wield their knives, their experience. They shuck ten to his one oyster and he wonders how it's possible. They shuck them and lay them out on the rock salt without losing a drop of the juice. Even with three-year-olds running past them and tugging at them and screaming at the top of their lungs and crying and fighting over slobbery dog toys. His mother and his aunt don't lose a drop of juice. He is amazed by his mother, but doesn't say so, never will again. And he will forget this moment the instant he leaves the room. Only somewhere—at a funeral, in a boardroom, on a mountaintop—sometime later will the image come back to him and he will be watching again, seeing his mother at the sink shucking oysters.

The oysters marinate for twenty minutes.

But no one waits.

Mrs. Roth goes out to the yard, kicks the soccer ball one time, runs after it, hard, fast, then says nothing but picks up the black-and-white ball and turns back. The children follow her across the lawn, leaping, jumping, trying to grab the ball back before she gets into the house, into the bathroom, where they swarm around her holding their cupped hands up, waiting their individual turns for two squirts of the fun foam soap.

They know the rules. So Mrs. Roth makes no announcement about how the soccer ball will wait in a newspaper basket on top of the TV until everyone's eaten.

Mrs. Swindan can't be bothered right now. She is swirling her hands in the jelly roll pan, smoothing out an inch-deep layer of coarse sea salt. "Just get another bottle from the garage," she says as she scours half the oyster shells and nests them in the salt. Mrs. Roth wraps each fresh oyster in a streaky rasher from the deli downtown and lays it out in a shell. Mrs. Hamel drizzles a mixture of white wine, hot sauce, garlic, and parsley over the shells. Half go out onto Mr. Roth's grill. Half go under the broiler in the kitchen.

The neighbors, talking loudly after all the mai tais, white wine, and sangria, line up, each with a heavy paper plate.

Summer sets in. Mrs. Swindan calls Christa over to the oven. There is no ceremony, no kneeling knightship, no rite of passage for a warrior in the woods, no moment of hesitation at all. Just, "Here. Take this out." So as instructed, the young new wife of one of the older grandchildren carries the most important platter to the table, elbows her way through the line of neighbors, and there are the angels on horseback, between the deviled eggs and Mrs. Hamel's Christmas fruit salad.

SMILES

Sometimes you are standing in line at the bank. And you smile because you feel you must. You don't expect to chat and converse but the teller is an old enemy from high school. You already know her story. You've heard five different versions of it. Worse. She knows yours.

You're in hot-pink sweatpants from Victoria's Secret. They're pulled up to mid-calf. And you don't remember in the moment that they were buy-one-get-a-free-purse-sized-perfume. You're wearing flip-flops with a row of rhinestones passing over the tan you rubbed on your feet, your belly, your shoulders, your legs. Your mother, every mother you know, used to say, "You can be anything, honey." She used to say, "We don't quit." Now she says, "I don't think you heard me the first time. I don't care who he is."

Your hair is a mess. And who gives a shit? It's ninety degrees and humid. You really weren't planning on seeing anyone anyway. Definitely not this chick.

Dammit. There's no avoiding her. She's already seen you and the other lady must be at lunch. You're next. You're waiting for your turn to reach out and grab a sucker from the baseball-shaped ceramic mug. You're behind the overweight guy in Wranglers, a dusty blue flannel work shirt, and big, red, wide suspenders. So what if she's looking at you, trying to wave a little bit, craning her neck around Mr. Can't-Wear-A-Belt-Like-A-Normal-Person to say hi before he's finished his business? Just stare all you want at the one brass clip on his waistband, which is slowly letting go of that denim edge. Metal fatigue, probably. The thing's got no grip left. It's gonna pop at any moment.

Your mother used to say, "Quit staring."
But why should you? That thing is barely holding
on and you want to see it spring loose the next
time he heaves with one of those COPD coughs.
What's the point of looking away? What's the deal
with all this shame, all this pretending nothing's
happening, all this putting a good face on a whole
bunch of bullshit? And why should you do it for
this guy in suspenders or for the old enemy from
high school who counts a stack of twenties and
keeps starting over? It's not pride or social
etiquette. It is not prayer—that's elsewhere. There
is no reason to pray for this girl or some old, fat
guy with red suspenders. So just keep looking at
that brass clip, which will definitely pop before he
gets back to his truck, and let your mind start its
usual subservient free fall.

You see that real unnamed breath, which
never has explained itself. As if you care. You
violently toss away your Bible school-issue halo
but it boomerangs, chokes you, and spins around
your neck like a fast, accurate horseshoe on a
stake cemented against the force of arthritic

clapping and victorious shouts by some great-uncle at a family reunion. And with this kind of physical proximity to the essence of life you know instantly and then know nothing of it, remembering the bank teller, this old enemy from high school, is divorced with two kids.

You should have just deposited this thing at the ATM but you can't now. You want a pineapple sucker and need a roll of quarters anyway. You shift your weight to place your body under the air conditioning vent. The man in the suspenders is finished with his business. He pounds a stack of envelopes on the counter and explains himself as he heads for the door, the truck, and the post office, which is under review. "Wouldn't have even had either overdraft fee if the payroll service didn't take the day off for the Fourth. Damn thing's automated. How's a computer gonna take the day off?" And he's gone.

The door is made of glass tinted brown.

Before you take that last step forward there is another glimmer in your mind but it is nothing fearful, nothing really intimidating, nothing that can hurt you. Not anymore. Those glimmers are good. They breed humility in your worldview, deference in decision-making, caution while driving, and hesitation in what you say. They are visitors that beguile certainty on tired afternoons, trespassers and traitors, like old friends lost, like space invaders.

But whatever. You don't have to look over your shoulder anymore. Just put your paycheck between your teeth, pull the boomerang/horseshoe/halo thing away from your throat, and readjust your headband. You don't have a duty to listen to this girl's sob story while she cashes your check.

You don't have to care. You don't. But you do need a roll of quarters. So you take that last step forward and smile. Just hand her the stupid paycheck and say it. "Hey. Girl. How've you been doing?"

You pick up the baseball-shaped coffee mug and start rifling through it looking for what you want.

She takes it as her cue to say she's recovering slowly from a bout of too much drinking which came out in the custody hearing—it's not as if she drives into oncoming traffic every day—but luckily they found in her favor. You do not care. But you still smile. So she goes on. She couldn't believe that the judge let him get out of paying the child support he'd missed: the child will only eat brand-name chicken nuggets, which are not cheap even if you buy in bulk. She moved back home with her mom and dad. They're helping her get on her feet again. She had to sell the house but that was okay because the roof needed to be replaced and the people that bought it knew some great roofers. She couldn't have afforded to put a roof on that house after all the court costs and divorce and all. But she's doing really well.

It's over. You've got the quarters. You've listened to whatever she felt the need to share. You're done. You turn to leave. You take a step away from the counter and have your sunglasses

back on before she says, "And what about you?
Did you decide to press charges?"

CHARACTER SKETCH, 1997

She had to have it, you know? That was
kind of her thing, real grabby-like.

But she was good at things that didn't rely
on others. She was good at things for a little while
and then moved on. She was good at things like
mixing drinks and cooking; like making jewelry;
arranging patio furniture under the setting Texan
sun; gardening, tomatoes mainly; and playing
video games. It's not like she was neat or
whatever. But she liked things a certain way in a
certain place and organized her CDs, rearranged
the inside furniture, too. Alphabetized books on
shelves. Stuff like that, you know. What else? Oh.

She was really good at picking songs and burning homemade compilations for friends. Crafts, too. She made envelopes, you know. Herself. By hand. Same with cigarettes and decoupage collages.

Yeah. I can tell you more. There's always more.

Mixing drinks: In a dinged-up, second-hand vase on the counter behind the sink she kept long glass swizzle sticks with bright ornamental figures on the tops. Hand-blown, you know? A monkey. A parrot. A palm tree. And a bright umbrella. They were a set. An expensive set of artisan-made swizzle sticks. Kitschy but beautifully rendered. They were precious to her and for fun she screamed at her friends, insisting they be careful with them too. It was like a joke, but super mean. Disrespectful. Matronizing. She didn't care. She made countless drinks in the kitchen. Tom Collins. Mint Julep. Gimlet. Clamato and Spicy Tequila with Lime Juice. Stirred them with the handle end of a broken knife she could not care less about, and then served them on the patio wearing their god-damn-it-don't-break-those swizzle sticks, expecting comment.

Cooking: She always used the right implement or pot for its express purpose. And she didn't mind the cleanup that this involved. She didn't mind at all. I know because she always told me, "I don't mind."

Making jewelry: She had a red Sears Craftsman toolbox where she kept all her jewelry-making supplies. The burliness was explained away. It was a really satisfying toolbox. In the top she kept all the beads in a carefully-organized removable tray. Underneath there were different wires and clasps and pairs of needle-nose pliers and graduated sizes of similar-looking tools. In the bottom of her butch jewelry-making box she also kept a paring knife. It had belonged to her great-grandfather who had come to America from Sweden via Ellis Island. She said he carved his initials in a lot of walls with that knife. She told the story saying she didn't approve of graffiti.

Gardening: Her garden was a tribute to her favorite architects. Bamboo structures were everywhere. She grew tomatoes on all of them except for the ones where peppers and sweet sugar snap peas with their "Awwww-look-aren't-they-sweet?" blossoms grew. But like Monet with his haystacks she had a focus and was mainly interested in the best structure to support tomatoes. Tried different things. Pyramids. Towers. Conical funnels. And round cages. She built whimsical bent-bamboo tomato trellis forts. After trying everything she found that an igloo-type structure provided the best support and ease of harvest for the tomatoes. It optimized the exposed surface area of the leaves to bright midday sunlight.

Video Games: She was very good at video games that involved racing. She could even race the game itself on the most difficult and trying courses. She was, however, not so good at the video games that involved the martial arts. Her roundhouse kick was a personal embarrassment.

Organizing CDs: If a friend were depressed and there seemed no way to contribute, she would show up on a breezy Saturday and organize the CDs as if of course that would help. She put them in genres—not in alphabetical order like the books. And once finished she put the DVDs and videotapes away. And she would look under the sink and put order there. Then she would make sure that the clothes in closets were not chaotic but pleasantly satisfying, orderly. She'd make a joke from a movie about wire hangers. After that, she would link her arm in her friend's arm and they would find a place to eat tamales and chicken wings outside in the afternoon. "You'll love it. Their cheladas are great."

Arranging the Furniture: The furniture in her living room was always a little discordant. She liked to have the bright yellow chaise next to her black metal apothecary chest right in front of the door as one walked in. It had an interesting effect. Not exactly feng shui. Coming into the room one was accosted by the fortress of furniture. But she had it that way for a reason. The person lying on the chaise could reach over and open the door without getting up. If the cops came, well, it bought time.

Burning Songs: She was a fanatic with the CD burner. But she made it a moral point to buy exactly one quarter of the downloaded artists' songs.

Making envelopes: The artisan envelope was her signature. When she sent invitations for her cocktail parties, which she had on the patio with citronella torchlight, low funky music, and those fancy blown-glass swizzle sticks that she yelled at her friends to use with care, she made the invitation envelopes herself out of old wrapping paper or wallpaper samples. But the effort was so great that the guest lists stayed short.

Rolling Cigarettes: She was very good at rolling cigarettes. She could do it in her hands. Or she could do it on her little cigarette-rolling machine that she took with her to diners late at night. Mostly it was tobacco.

Collages and Decoupage: She collected pieces of wood. Mainly small, really quite useless cutting boards. She never used wooden cutting boards in her kitchen. Didn't like bacteria to breed at an uncontrollable rate. But they were such beautiful pieces of wood, those little cutting boards. So she bought them, the smallest ones, the most useless ones, whenever she got the chance. She cut pictures of thin-armed girls in well-suited homes from magazines. *Dwell. Better Homes & Gardens. National Geographic.* And *Surf Digest.* She made collages on the cutting boards with decoupage glue and a pair of really sharp haircutting scissors from the beauty supply shop.

Planting terrariums in perfume bottles: Though short-lived, for a time she made a hobby of planting terrariums in tiny perfume bottles. She made a great terrarium and gave it to her elderly neighbor whose children had decided to sell the old woman's house and move her into an assisted living community. Who could blame them for the market? Houses just wouldn't ever get these kinds of prices again. But still. It didn't seem right to sell an old lady's house out from under her without her consent. So my friend with the jewelry-making toolbox and the art glass swizzle sticks and the optimal bamboo structure for growing tomatoes stayed up all night and planted a teeny tiny terrarium for her neighbor to take with her to her last new life.

Humming: But. You know how things go. There are ups and downs. Not everything is the way you might hope. My friend was just like anyone that way. She panicked. She threw things. She shoved people. She held close friends in vicious contempt. She was paranoid. She didn't care. She was defensive. She was wounded. She was on drugs but not like they teach you in school. She was above all that and did drugs for fun, for freedom, for something to do with her disposable income, for the hell of it, for the experience, for enough quality bonding time, for better sex, for enlightened transcendence and Whip-it! laughs. Sometimes she cried and screamed with an infantile sense of injustice. But. Whenever she was driving alone she was happy. And she hummed.

WHIMSY

Anyway, Milo decides we should crawl up the bar, over the curling roses in the woodwork, under that old blower they use to keep the smoke inhalation to a minimum, and just go right smack into the mirror.

It's an antique. I admit a fleeting moment of reservation. We'd been enjoying ourselves, chatting it up with an irascible sushi chef and the bartender. Not that one girl with curly hair but the skinny guy in belted black jeans. The one who always makes us listen to Kenny G. on Tuesday nights.

Conversation was enough for me. I didn't need the escalation but Milo seemed to know best.

Bitter glee, so unburdened by the fates as to seem almost, well, almost as if our youth did exist, replaced any notice of the passing time. So it didn't really matter that I was afraid. Milo climbed into the mirror demanding that I follow.

I don't blame him for not explaining more. Likely he didn't know what either of us was about to get into, couldn't have foreseen. But he seemed so experienced that he might have mentioned what would happen when our dives began.

Although, really, I forget myself and am not sure I can describe it all that well, not from the very beginning. Glass is an amorphous solid, a sort of impossible-to-perceive liquid. I believed it wasn't substantial. Still I didn't know how fast, or how slowly, how thick or thin, how sick or healthily I would have to go on to move through such a strange seemingly-solid fluidity.

Oh. Wait. Now I remember Milo saying that diving down into the mirror felt like rolling through a roundness, hard and unfathomable, and it would almost be like sliding around the curve of one of those colored twists that stays, forever trapped, in a marble.

We each had our individual experiences but falling through the mirror happened to both of us simultaneously. There was no fun house displacement or condensation. He was not me; I was not him. We were one with the reflection.

Marbles don't shatter. They bounce and clatter. That's the kind of place it was. The world inside the mirror isn't really that different from a lakeside walk. It is darker, sure. But not all completely unfamiliar. It's not what I expected which was an underground mine that opens out like a tree fort made out of peaty stuff and branches into civic-planning-committee train stations on a mythological river, you know? Or an igloo. Or, no!, a cave, where water drips stalactite-ish, into calcified blue, artificially-lit pools of well-marketed discovery. And it's not hot, either. I'm

not sure what it's like exactly. You'll have to ask
Milo.

But however it was there was no oxygen,
so at one point, with self-preservation in mind, we
decided to just give up breathing, to conserve
what reserves we each had packed away deep
down in the alveolar recesses of all the
amorphous impossibility inside ourselves. (That
was my idea.) After a while we wanted so very
much to begin again with our lives the way they
had been that we tumbled so sleepy, like zoo-kept
belugas, against our window of the world. You
know the one. It's like the one at Rockefeller
Center, only bigger. Like, Grand Canyon big, only
glass.

I huddled with the masses. He nuzzled
like a baby calf, only tougher, more respectable.

When we woke (and don't ask me what
exactly happened, because I don't remember
everything and—thank God—neither does he)
there was something different. I felt sort of
crowded in a way that I didn't know before. I
stood up but found no internal way back out and

up through the liquid marble twist. We'd held off for a long time but used up our reserves. Breathing became necessary. I had to inhale something, didn't I? So I just took my surroundings in. It wasn't agony when I felt that marble twist fill my lungs. It was like lavender ornamental florist beads that put attractive weight in the bottom of a minimalist crystal vase to hold the flower stems just so.

I was completely committed. My chest filled with the weight.

I had been in love, twice, but had never been possessed to the point that I required exorcism. So, it was very odd to realize, to know, to become aware that we were the same human being, suddenly. It was all elbows and squished in.

We denied its influence, its very reality. There is something so unnecessary about a friend who actually lives in your entirety. Like a lifetime witness. I like Milo, don't get me wrong. And, to my knowledge, Milo's never once said a bad word about me. It is what it is, I guess. Just too much, too close.

So anyway, I stood there—right there
with him—trying to accept that we'd become one
being breathing twisted glass lung-filled
something against our reversing image window of
the world into and through all the me of him that
I never even tried to get used to.

THE SANDWICH

Stilled isolation and forgotten sock sounds make the harmony of my attempt at beginning.

I don't remember why but I guess a week ago a cop friend called my mother, said he was taking me to a hospital, a psych hospital. Mom came to visit. Felt she had to. Resented it. But. Came nonetheless. It was like usual. Five days to stabilize the meds, to ask all the right questions, to teach me to cope, again, to deal with my mother and the paperwork, and then to set me free as if my mind would allow it.

Mom left yesterday, which is fine.

How do you do your best to sort everything with a glued-back-together-and-held-by-vice-grips mind? You can't ask anyone for help with this part. No one knows what you mean. If they do know, they pretend ignorance. So just hush and hurry to fracture your constant stream with prism eyes as information comes sideways.

Inanimate things take their toll on me. My socks rest where they were left on an unremembered day. I think about my broken mind and try to let the glue dry. Let it harden while dealing with the coming of a teakettle in the apartment next door. Culling awareness, I put what I hear in different places with their pictures of female members of the family. Or men, sometimes, for the guy sounds. Distant traffic revving at the street light goes into a memory of the accidental night. Gasping hawks get put away with photographs of my father. Inside the socks lay crinkled on the couch and still. Weighing me down with their no-sound way to put them anywhere.

If the floor is, in fact, under the bed, it will not sink, I guess. But who can be sure where the floor ever is?

But if the floor is, in fact, under the bed, then I guess I am pretty hungry. Jell-O would be great. Knox Blox, to be exact. Cut out with nestable cookie cutters of different-sized stars. Slip yellow points into red corners and be good enough, be someone worthy, be happy to put one star inside the other like it shows how to do on the package. But you need vegetable oil that has no flavor to grease the perpendicular-pressure aluminum. I only have sesame oil. And I hate eating art.

So then what? Gravy? I don't know how to make gravy. What'll I do with the lumps? There will be lumps because I am not good enough to make anything come out right. I don't know how to make gravy or anything so they gave me a brochure about self-esteem and said to check a website once a week for coping tips. I can chat in real time with a trained counselor who's twenty-two and makes eight fifty an hour. Sometimes, even so, a yearning rises and grips my center, sending me into a kind of God-lust. Sometimes a yearning comes undone and drifts sideways, changing Mother's hand-me-down thoughts into a kind of almost-wonderland.

Life being half indebted inheritance and half unrealized potential, I am trying to resurface in an unrecognized welcome.

I am awash in similarity. I don't even have what-ifs. But whatever. Instead of getting anywhere with my vision of the meta-almosts I end up with all sorts of not-quite-good-enoughs and probably-could-have-beens and just give up buying anything with built-in obsolescence, like boyfriends and homes, though it seems there is nothing but continuing. No splendor. No deep roots. Simply the day-by-day inebriation of adulthood.

The church tears at the politician who shouts at the people and says, "Hope. Change." Change what? Hope for whom? Myself with others? My other realms with each other? You have got to be kidding. My rhythm of death-days has become so same, so unending, and I am succumbing to the trance of disbelief that shrouds nations.

But. It's okay. There's a pill for what ails me. Just do the laundry. Clean the bathroom. Hang the towels. Spray 409 on the stove. Water the plants. Go to the gym. Feed yourself. Clothe yourself. Take out the trash. Enjoy things like music, books, TV shows, and beach volleyball. Participate. Learn. Invest. Grow. Plan a trip to meet indigenous peoples in a rain forest and discuss intercultural affairs on an ecotourism adventure that's well-enough controlled to be both liberating and safe. Airplanes are natural. Drive your car. Don't let the gas tank get too low. Pay for things with cash. Live within your means. Hang up the clothes. Mop the floor. Do the dishes. Remember the import of eating a balanced diet, of exercise, of maintaining relationships, of having people over to smell your scented candles, to pet your dogs, to comment on your wall art, to play your piano, to rifle through your medicine cabinet, and to sit back down on your couch pretending nothing ever happened.

The house sits animated but still ready to pounce around me with its penetrating unspoken screams. Ready to emerge as *life moving on.*

Sandwich. Bread. Pepperidge Farm white bread. Fresh. Mayonnaise. Salt and pepper. Leftover baked rotisserie chicken breast. Lettuce. Not iceberg but romaine. Or buttercrunch, I think they call it. Tomato. No. Tomato on the side with more mayonnaise and salt and pepper.

The bed is moving. No. The walls are moving. No. It's the clouds outside the window streaming by. And the bed is dropping away through the floor I knew didn't really exist and couldn't.

I have to eat. That's what they say. "You have to eat." They say if you can feed yourself sufficiently then you don't have to go to strange places where the doors are heavier than the walls that ripple, haunted and waterlogged with similar muzzled lives. So different from seedy hotels. So same. So eat. I have to eat.

It's not pieces of your mind falling into shattered disarray again, unsortable. It's low blood sugar.

Sandwich. There must be a way.

Fight. Like Christina in Wyeth's muted grass world. Make your way to what you want, what you need, what you have to have. Make a well-deserved sustenance for yourself—your body and mind.

The store is only three blocks away. You can make it. You can do this alone. But is there any money? Under the table in the hall: don't you remember seeing a quarter? Yes. But that's been at least five years ago and it was at home in—well, wherever that was. But the floor was a cheap, lacquered jewelry box from Japan. A tourist trinket and black, almost, under that table. It was dark reddish-fade-to-black hardwood veneer that will never chip off. And the quarter was just there somehow in a beam of sunlight. And I saw it. I didn't pick it up. But I saw it there just like that under the foyer table on the souvenir floor. Still,

just like that years ago. But it wouldn't be enough
to take to the store today anyway.

Mom said there was money in a drawer.
She is always using drawers for things, like money,
that shouldn't be hidden, that need to be seen.

But pull yourself toward the creation of a
sustaining reality.

Commit to small certainties. The salt will
sit on the chicken breast and on the skin from the
rotisserie and you will just barely be able to see
how you've seasoned it.

I remember sandwiches like that.

I have to eat.

I will make a sandwich like that.

There are three dollars in my coat. I know
the money's there. Or at least I hope it is. Hope it
hasn't been changed. But it's probably there from
the time I bought cigarettes across the street.
Good. Yes. Here it is. It's real. I remembered it
right and I am holding it with two hands,
touching it, checking, counting, assuring myself
again, and counting again, but yes, it's here. It's
really here. This is one thing that's not an illusion,

an expectation, a hope, a change, a delusion, a hallucination, a must-have-remembered-it-wrong embarrassed moment, a confusion, a frustration, a trust, an unknowing, a worry, a panic, a thought-so-but-no. It's real.

So. I won. I'm fine. I remembered it right, which means it's real, I'm fine, and my broken brain didn't process it wrong. Not this time. This time I remembered it right. There was three dollars in my coat pocket. I was right. It's real. It's right here in my hand. It's real. I'm looking at it and it's here. I feel it and it's real.

So the coat and the drawer and as long as the floor is there again we're okay. We're okay and we're not going anywhere without shoes and a hat. Where is the hat? I guess it doesn't matter as long as I have the beach towel memory. The one with the dancing Planters peanut on it from all those lost beach summers. God. When will this glue dry? I need to find my hat. I don't need to remember a twenty-year-old, navy blue, dancing top-hat-and-cane monocled-peanut towel on a clotheslined breeze.

Just focus and find the floor. Test it for rotten spots with your leading toe.

The coat. The drawer. The door. The stairs. And another door to the porch. Fine. I'm okay. I'm okay. Just act normal. No one even knows. No one even knows. No one even knows. No one can see your glazed-cherry-blossom-broken-vase glue drying or all the brain pieces held in place so carefully with direct pressure. Just keep walking. Just be careful. Do everything the right way. Look both ways. Cross the street when other people cross the street. Give up when no one else seems to care. Just relax. Relax. There is nothing emotional or psychological or pathological or anything that needs psychiatric care between here and the grocery store. The sidewalk can't do that. It didn't. So breathe in again and just keep going. Sidewalks don't move. Just keep going. Breathe out again and don't worry. It didn't happen.

It might just be the pills.

Did I take my pills? Did I take them? Or was that this morning? Or yesterday? Or did the

pills go through the wall to the teakettle sound
where the floor fell down into the sinkhole of a
grass world impossible to traverse while dragging
two crippled limbs across the field of color that
must be carpet hanging like a pet-door trap that
keeps out the elements with the help of towels on
clotheslines and quarters and breeze under foyer
tables on jewelry box floors from five years ago?

Just keep walking.

Don't hold your breath. Don't panic.
Don't worry. Don't cry. Just keep walking.

Nothing's happening. Everything's fine.
Everything's normal. There's no problem.

And some people do understand. A lot of
people have been through this. There were plenty
of people in that hospital. This is not just you.
You're just the only one in your head. But you're
not the only one who this has ever happened to.
So. Breathe. Relax. Understand the biochemistry,
the physiology, the genetics, the statistics, the
probabilities, the diagnoses, the family history, the
reasons why.

I remember someone's telling me about a huge revolving door in a supermarket with a tank of fish in the middle. The tank is drained now. Broken. I wonder how they drained it. Hope the fish got out okay.

Don't worry about that. That doesn't matter. It's not related. The money is real and it's related to the sandwich parts you still need.

Grocery store. The fruit is amazing, isn't it? Isn't it? Where does it all come from? All this fruit to all these grocery stores. Can it possibly be used, all this fruit? It can't possibly be consumed. I guess it just goes on sale. Is that it? It's not like the bins of screws at the hardware store. These rot.

Don't waste your time reading little stickers of distant provenance and feeling sorry for soft mangoes.

Mayonnaise. I don't know where it is. Where is it? Bread. And how about pickles? Yes, pickles. There is definitely enough money with the coat and the drawer.

Don't wander. If you can't find the bread, go back to the produce section and start over. Just go up and down all the aisles. Focus. Concentrate. You're looking for bread.

See? There it is. That's where the bread is. That's how you do it. That's how you find things you know must be there.

You're done. Now. Go pay.

Smile at the lady. Just smile at the lady. Pretend. It's all just pretend. Smile again.

Don't look through her. She'll know.

Say, "Thank you. Have a nice day." And say it like no awareness is cascading over you.

Push. Don't panic. Fish don't matter.

The sky seems more.

Back to the house. Back to the house. Back to the house. And breathe. Breathe. If you know it, they know it. So just breathe. Breathe. Carry the bag and breathe.

Up the stairs. There is a lock on the door but the key is here somewhere. I live here so it's okay. I have the key. That's allowed. So go ahead, just ease on in.

Sit.

Okay.

Sit. Sandwich.

But the knife. No way. Not today. Just fingers today. Just pull the chicken apart. And use a spoon for the mayonnaise. It's good enough. No knife. Not today. Maybe next time, but not today. Knives are too full of potential. Too easy to take off fingers and toes. Too easy to pull the skin off shins and ankles. Too easy to peel away the eyelids and soft places next to the ears. And so not today. Use the spoon today. Ignore the tremor.

Salt.

Pepper.

And pickles, sitting in the chair by the window.

Finally.

JULY & THE BUFF ORPINGTONS

Before their necks are broken they are
beautiful. These chickens live under a tent for a
week in July. The heat wraps up and around the
sides of the tent and hangs thick in the middle.
The day is hot but it is hotter inside the tent even
with its shade. The bird cages are steel mesh wire.
Not big, flimsy hexagons but little, tight squares
less than half an inch across. At the places where
the wires cross over each other the metal is built
up. There is a matte coating over it that hides the
welds. Slow, scaly feet move easily over the open-
work wires but are careful, intentional.

The fans are humming. They are old and rattling—real metal fans that hang in four corners of the tent. The air is heavy and even these industrial fans are ridiculous against such weight. Smells circulate but air barely moves with the fans' futility. It is so hot for the birds that someone, some thoughtful caretaker, brought a plastic home-use fan. Everyone has a fan like this. It's the kind that sits on dingy golden carpet in hallways, by sunken couches in living rooms, on cherry veneer tables beside beds where love gets made, and on top of endlessly-flashing-noon-'cause-no-one-knows-how-to-reset-the-time microwaves in disinfected kitchens. So, having seen such fans everywhere else, it's not so strange to see one in the poultry tent. Someone has pushed the darkest brown button and pulled the white peg up so the fan will oscillate on top of the middle row of cages. As the fan directs and redirects its effort, pink, purple, blue, and white ribbons sing out, fluttering enough to draw attention to particular cages. Those wire rooms for the birds are lined up as a single-file perimeter around the sides of the tent and two deep back-to-back down the center. Observers flow as if channeled through thick-walled ventricles of a heart.

Feathers move slightly as the fans push the air. There are bits of feathers gathered down around the wooden stilt-legs of the cages on the limestone gravel. There are feathers in the fans. And feathers in the cages. And feathers in the taut fraying jute ropes of the tent. Just downy white and gray pieces mostly. The few good, big, pretty, golden feathers are picked up quickly and swept away to shaft-stroking wonderlands with the giggles of little girls.

The chickens pick up their bony, intentional feet and slow-dance, sometimes even with flapping wings. They turn and their feet seem backwards. Then, not forgotten, the bodies turn. With short jolts, their heads betray nothing held in confidence. The eyes focus and then turn away. Strangers read names of the owners out loud and point, showing each other whatever they see as important. We do it, too. "Come over here and look at this one."

For twenty years my mother has taken me and my father to the fair. We go through the sheep barn. We go through the cattle barns, dairy and beef. We look up at the names painted on the rafters: names of friends, and brothers of friends, and fathers of friends. Green paint on old white paint. We remember our head, our heart, our hands, and our health. Sandals fill with dust as we walk down the missing-lightbulb midway. We eat something familiar because it's only once a year. There is no anxiety for goldfish swimming through food-color-dyed waters in dirty bowls and no mortal fear for the cheap stuffed nothings everyone wants to win.

We wander slowly through it all. It is hot, July. We stop. I want to watch the boys throwing darts at a rainbow wall of slack balloons. Because there is no sense of impending doom for that child who paid for his three chances. He aims while my father crosses his arms over his chest and stares. We feel the imminent impact. We want

the child to perform well, to win the biggest, best
prize: the huge stuffed tiger. But who can really
hope for so much? And what responsibility does
this child have to our family? None. So. We don't
really care if the child bursts something nothing-
filled. We don't expect it. The first dart glances
off the pulverized wooden board and drops into a
metal collecting tray. He refocuses. Aims again.
Then one, two steel darts pop big yellow flopping
balloons as we cheer, congratulate, and smile. The
child turns to us and smiles too. Dad walks on.
We follow.

It cannot be that this will kill him. I look
at my father, who stands with us eating a pork
burger from the Rotary Club's tent. He watches
the people walk by. He speaks to the ones he
knows. They don't know yet, but we know. And
still we smile and say hello. We laugh at the
round-bellied kid in the little red tee shirt. And we
ask the questions that you ask. But we don't say,
"He's dying." We will have to soon enough.

We walk through the barns where my
projects once were. Barns I remember cleaning on

cold spring days when you shouldn't really use a hose yet. Barns I remember hiding in. At five and fifteen. They still smell the same. Hay. Dirt. Sunshine. Cement. And Time. No one savors moments like this, moments when you share personal speculations about who will probably win in all the baked goods categories. So. We wander over to the show ring.

The hogs fill up the arena. We laugh at the smallest children showing the comparatively huge animals. They rush around the ring in their little Wranglers, boots, and tucked-in dress shirts. But we don't laugh at their age or stature. We laugh in appreciation of their competence. They know everything about showing hogs: shine them; tap them with the little whips; keep the hogs between their bodies and the judges; move the animals along quickly so their ears flop and their haunches bounce on coquettish trotting hooves; and always keep both eyes right on that judge.

We all fall in love with one tiny skinny boy in particular, because he's so focused, so intent, so practiced, so self-assured, so competitive.

He will grow up here, that boy showing those hogs. Knowing how. But we all grew up here. Not Mom. Not Dad. But the rest of us. The woman leaning over the fence grew up here. The man sitting next to me grew up here. I grew up here.

And so I know everything that happens in this ring. There are auctions. There are dances. There are obstacle course races where greased-up kids hold greased-up watermelons and go under bales of hay, through kiddie pools of water, and shimmy around poles to ride scale-model tricycle-tractors towing stacked cinder blocks on skids. Fair Queen pageants go on here where girls win and girls lose. But today it is the hogs oiled up and glittered in the ring looking very good and showing off.

The judging is over and there won't be anything else going on in the ring for a while. So we head back towards the car but stop. Mom wants to walk through the poultry tent. So we do. The birds are preposterous. They are amazing forms of life. They are beautiful and clean and cocky. Before their necks are broken.

She never asked to move here.

"The Buff Orpingtons are my favorite," she says. She holds his hand. And she knows that he's dying. And she knows the chickens are dying. And she was still careful to park in the shade in July.

AN ADMISSIONS ESSAY

I am really interested in attending your university. Well. Not really. But. I have a passable—check that—I have a socially acceptable amount of interest in doing what it takes to get by. Of course I care just enough to write this the day before the deadline. Well. Okay. Fine. Two hours before the deadline.

Anyway. Steve Cohen says when writing this kind of essay, *"Whenever possible, kids should stay away from the 3-Ds—death, disease, and divorce."* I don't see why. It's like you're supposed to prove your worth and inner fortitude by talking about shit that doesn't matter at all. I mean, yes, good, great, awesome: I was captain of the lacrosse team. Who wasn't? Do you care? No.

The point is, last year, on the day that my mother and father were both killed in a head-on collision while coming home from the dissolution hearing that ended their marriage, I, having recently been informed (two hours previously) that I was now head of household, received a phone call from my extended family's internist who went into great detail about my grandmother's imminent demise.

I didn't want to step up. What the fuck? But the doctor's sense of urgency moved me, and—given the gravity of the situation—I felt strongly that Grandmother should not hear about the extremity of her diagnosis over the phone. She turns her ringer off during *Wheel of Fortune* anyway so calling her wasn't an option.

I couldn't drive over to Grandma's to inform her of the dire situation as the family car was totaled. In fact, after being described in a police report and being photographed by the insurance agent, the gruesome mangle of crunched plastic and metal was still being hosed down so it could be towed off to the junkyard after the (Awful! Pitiable! Just terrible!) wreck that killed my parents.

Usually I just let Grandma watch her shows. I don't go over there. Why would I? But. Come on. She had a right to know what I knew after the doctor told me what was going on with my family that was so quickly falling apart. So. That day, instead of forgetting about my grandmother and biding the allotted half-hour during which *Wheel of Fortune* airs, instead of chatting about the rather widespread use of inhalants, I got on my bike and headed over to her house.

I read online that, "According to a 2002 AARP report, approximately 50 percent of grandparents live more than 200 miles from their grandchildren." In our family, on average, the distance is 780 miles because there's so much circuitous evasion and avoidance between my parents' and her place. That day I settled for less than average, made a beeline on my bike, and it was closer.

By the time I got there, she was dead. I wasn't sure exactly what to do. The coroner's cell number was in my phone from the events of the morning. I sent him a text asking if he wouldn't mind to swing by, pick her up, and drop g'ma over to the funeral home, too.

It was a tough day. I'm not sure why it makes me want to go to college or why I'm sending this essay to your particular institution of exorbitantly expensive post-secondary education, but I guess I just feel like maybe I can hang out with the cool kids there, drink some beer, and hopefully get to use your quantum harmonic oscillator sometimes.

DEBRIEFING

Every Friday before they released us to go buck wild after being oppressed all week they debriefed us. I stood at parade rest with the other soldiers. We sweated through our BDUs in the Texas heat and endured a suicide lecture.

Imagine a little, tiny, drowned-rat-looking-mustached, bourbon-skinned drill sergeant standing at the front of the company. He kicks the cement, shakes his head, paces. The rant ends with, "There's always a solution. You might not like the solution. But there's a solution."

Then, after the week's recap, he screams at all of us. "Do not trucking kill yourselves this weekend! I do not want to have to call your momma. No motel maid needs to deal with finding your head exploded in the bedsheets. And I'm not going to do the dang-blasted paperwork. So if you get any trucking ideas about breaking into the ammunition shed, or hanging yourself in a hotel room, or slitting your wrists in the shower bays, think again!

"You will be here Monday morning. You will stand up. You will be counted."

That's what he said.

MA DEUCE

That summer night, before I joined the army, I thought swimming would mean we'd hop a fence in some Canadian neighborhood. But no. We drove out onto a back road and then further down a rutted grass path covered with trees until the guy's car gave up and stopped.

I was drunk enough. As soon as I got out of that car I heard the roar, saw low orange clouds. Two guys, boys really, took us down a path to some sort of trestle or crane that reached out over the Niagara River. Now I don't know the exact distance we were upstream from the falls. But I know the river was already anxious about going over that edge. Swift currents rushed over rocks. Eddying shifting waters surged in smooth swells nearby. Right under the trestle the water was just one smooth silk curl and deep enough. If I had to guess conservatively, I'd say we were less than a mile upstream from the falls. I shudder to think how close we really were.

Civilization now has nothing to do with simpering sets of crossed ankles and ungloved fingers reaching for tea cakes. A woman has only to do with regulations. It's a life of don'ts. One can only stand so long at a kitchen sink, pouring simple glasses of homemade lemonade. Such god damned relegation. A woman is not to enjoy standing under some inundating Niagara, or to love the concussion of the falls, to feel the doom-damning imminent thrill of maybe, just maybe, accidentally going over the falls.

No one should, I guess. It's not about equal rights anymore. It's really more a safety concern. Still I think, "But what of Liberty?"

A more secure woman wouldn't have joined the army, but I did and stood in a tiny little shed above the night-fire course in the Ozarks. I was with a drill sergeant who manned a machine gun. He shot live rounds out over the soldiers from my platoon, friends, who were low-crawling under barbed wire getting tear gas powder in their mouths. I backed into the corner of the shed and watched the shell casings pile up on the floor. He said to me, "Jones. You're one of those serious privates, aren't you?"

I had a huge crush on this guy. He was hot, skinny, rugged, and drove a cherry red classic convertible Mustang from the '60s. But when he said to me, "Jones. You're one of those serious privates, aren't you?" while magnesium flares burst over the live-fire training field where two hundred of my friends were, that crush ended.

I agreed, I suppose. Who knows?

Not then but later, I thought back to the night I jumped into the Niagara River so close to those falls. Before deciding to go for a swim with the guys we met, this friend and I went out after her mom had gone back to the hotel. We met the guys at the bar. They followed us onto the street.

Then we all four wandered. You know, somewhere together with nowhere in mind. I don't remember climbing onto the roof of a grocery store. But we did and tossed rocks near the feet of unsuspecting pedestrians. You'd toss a stone and then watch a woman look all around for the culprit. Invariably, she'd never look up. Women don't. We did not throw rocks at men.

Anyway, after we grew tired of this grocery store roof game, one of the guys must have said, "You girls want to go swimming?"

So what if I was a serious private a few months later?

Who knows who jumped from the trestle first, but when it was my turn I fell somewhere between ten and thirty feet to the water. That stupendous current accepted my body like nothing ever had. I swam like crazy for the bank. I think my friend may have jumped more than once, but I'm pretty sure that once was enough for me. I knew I'd reached some kind of limit of my daring. I don't think I was the only one. After a couple of jumps each we found what privacy was available as couples and made out on the high cement pylons.

The drill sergeant ended up disgusted with me in that machine gun shed a few months later and seemed to feel I'd ruined his evening with my thoughtful awareness. Canadian boys on cement pylons are one thing. But it might have been nice to end up making out with this hot drill sergeant in the little shed with that .50 caliber machine gun. Instead he was all pissed off about me being so serious, so aware of bullets ripping out pieces of the sky. I didn't apologize. What had I done but stare grieving into the night?

I accidentally stepped backwards onto his hat when my feet were almost covered in shell casings. That did it. He could never forgive me now.

At the river above the falls, I can't remember the structure we were on, not really. I've tried to revisit the place in my mind, but there are only puzzle pieces that don't fit well with lemonade glasses in hospitable hostess hands or with feet burning in sun-penetrating spit-shined

Airborne boots. But I remember falling from a
rusted, jagged, abandoned metal transom jutting
out over the water from two huge cement pylons.
I remember going down, down, deep down,
under an orange sky cloud-filled. Those
obfuscating cumulus vapors lay lowered right on
top of the sodium lights and roar.

GRAND PRIX PARALLELS

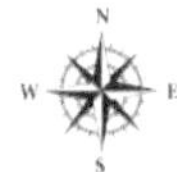

Boys of the rich, sit.

Powdery gold eyes

shadowed by a man at the door,

by hats, and scaring us all

left vintage prey, and

shadowed by a cheap night riot.

Boys of the rich, sit.

Boys of the poor, look,

far away fun. The flesh seared to

a cookout afternoon. And then

open. Their hearts perforated

skeleton shells, eaten through working

virtue, easy-for-me, eyes.

Boys of the rich, sit while

boys of the poor, look, fuckable poor,

clutching sweaty drunk fists, and

by parasite faith I am the pretty

listener today for one man

playing fool-fueled

balcony games on a

cookout grill, chatting weather

stories, for me.

Not achievement, or politics, or

blood-borne fights. Just girls,

girls, girls, ugly fuckable girls, and beer.

And his disposable expense of

how (craning and wide)

I was the pretty attendant for the

sweet regular boy, who cooked

quiet and calm, with the drunken wet

(beer, beer, ugly fuckable beer)

glass shattered in patient hands.

Holding (no money wads in pockets, just)

the shards and blood alike

And proud he excused himself

(ugly, sweet)

to clean up the mess

kissing me gently on the way.

JEANIE

Girls with something to prove aren't the best to fall in love with. The best type of girl to fall for is one who has given up altogether—a girl who wants nothing and can't remember if she ever cared anyway. The best type of girl, if you're looking for girls, is a girl who can offer you only herself. You'll know when you meet her. She'll have hollow eyes and never enough to do. But not everyone listens, and sometimes a girl, a stubborn and beautiful girl, gets herself fallen in love with. And then I say, pitying, pompous, loving, kind: *Why don't you ever listen?*

"No. I don't want to, and I won't." Her childhood bedroom door muffled Jeanie's voice.

Her mother held the locked doorknob and leaned heavily against the door, hoping pressure might help her reach her daughter. "But he's come all this way, sweetheart. Don't you want to talk to him? Hear him out?" There was only silence. After a minute her mother heard a page turn. Her daughter was reading and relaxed with no intention of speaking to anyone.

Mrs. B. turned slowly in the hall trying to come up with the right words to offer this young man with his earnest intentions. She didn't want to see his face again. No one had expected him from the way Jeanie made things sound, and yet here he was. He drove over two days to face a family that hated him and a girl who didn't want to open her door. It wasn't right. Mrs. B. pictured the poor boy waiting in the living room. His eyes filled with misunderstanding. His limbs loose and unwanted. His hair meant that he had given up and his smile was too vigorous.

Mrs. B. slipped her hands into the pockets of her apron and leaned back against the hallway wall. Her head knocked a picture frame and she sprang away to prevent it from falling. As it swung on the tiny nail, she looked at the picture. It was from some professional photography studio. Jeanie was two or three in the picture and smiling brightly into the dark hallway across time. Mrs. B. remembered fighting and piling everyone into the car that day. Jeanie had cried all the way to the studio and all the way home, but for a few minutes under the big silver umbrellas of light, which intimidated some of the most brave children, Jeanie basked happily, smiling, and cooing for the camera.

The picture was beginning to turn yellow.

Next to it there was a shot of Jeanie in ballet. She was third from the end in a long row of Saturday morning ballerinas. The other thin little figures stood with their feet together and their arms at their sides. Among them, Jeanie stood resolutely with her arms thrown open and her feet planted wide apart. None of the girls was over six years old, and Jeanie was certainly one of the smaller ones, but somehow the command of her stance filled her smiling mother with courage. It was impossible to know what was going on that moment, whether Jeanie were stretching, behind a step, or just plain ignoring directions, but the picture led one to believe that it was Jeanie, little tiny round-bellied Jeanie, who was bounds ahead of the rest and quickly catching on to the newest motion.

It's probably more foolish for a bunch of little girls from a nowhere town to ever think they could become ballerinas than for them to believe in Santa Claus. But then it's even funnier that mothers and aunts go on encouraging hopes of *Nutcracker* stardom long after Santa Claus and the Tooth Fairy become the silly forgotten nonsense of childhood.

The next picture showed Jeanie with her brothers and sisters and a number of other children at the beach. Her mother remembered the day. Jeanie had organized every child in a two-mile radius into an elaborate game. There were children running along a jetty diligently scraping barnacles and directing the water traffic. There were children pulling beach grass and raking seaweed into enormous piles that other children were building into fortresses. There were children who ran, children who cleared rocks, and children who defended boulders. There were children making piles of clam shells, and mussel shells, and there were children grinding the shells, in exact proportions, into a medicinal slag with rounded stones in the bottoms of six brightly-colored pails. There were children clearing the ravine of the sharpest rocks, and children screaming to one another from king-of-the-mountain vantage points. There were two tiny children looking for live periwinkles for the sake of an activity, and there were some bigger children who stood awkwardly nearby, wishing they were younger so as to be less inhibited and more involved. No one understood the rules. Jeanie was at the center of it all and the children swarmed around her looking for tactical advice, reassurance, a reassessment or clarification of the rules, and guidance. They brought their products for her approval and asked her to mull over this or that strategy and plan.

Most of the children were running nonstop the entire morning but Jeanie sat in her emerald green suit and dark tan on top of a rock dictating the show and making sure to include everyone. When no one needed her she sat looking at the water. Sometimes she looked out at the horizon with conviction. Sometimes she looked down into the shadow of the rock and watched the clinging seaweed thrash in the water. Mrs. B. remembered so much motion from those hours of that day but in the picture Jeanie's little feet were drawn up close to her body. Amid the ocean and the swarm of children she was tiny. Waves crashed all around the huge rock.

To get the best picture, her mother had strolled up, in the way that mothers sometimes do in their broad-brimmed hats, and dropped in to visit the self-appointed queen. When she asked her daughter to explain the game, Mrs. B. remembered Jeanie's saying to her, from behind Mickey Mouse sunglasses, "It's like war, Mommy.

No one understands it, so someone just has to pretend so that nobody will be scared. Then everyone will be okay." The game ended late in the day when the troops were exhausted and the queen's throne was overcome by the tide. Even when every child on the beach fights as hard as any full-grown squadron can, they don't defeat the tide.

There were other pictures on the wall but Mrs. B. looked past them and let her eyes rest on another one of Jeanie. She was onstage lighting a candle. It was the honor society induction ceremony her freshman year of high school. No one in the family had heard about the upcoming event. There was no mention of it from Jeanie. Mr. B. had been reading the paper and saw his own daughter's name among those listed to be honored that evening. Confounded, frustrated, confused, he stood up and wandered into the utility room where Mrs. B. was folding towels. He read the article aloud to his wife and then stared at her. It was close to six o'clock. The paper said the ceremony started at seven thirty. They had decided to confront their child with the paper and had gone together down this hall to their daughter's door to ask Jeanie about it. She said that, yes, she was being inducted but that she didn't understand why they had to make a big deal out of it. There was no reason to go. She didn't feel like going. Mr. B. said he didn't really care what she felt like and that it wasn't her decision to make. This had escalated to a loud altercation mainly between Mr. B. and Jeanie.

At seven fifteen the whole family was in the van and they were all in foul moods. There were several complaints of hunger, as dinner was left in cold pots on the stove. B comes early in the alphabet so they hurried. Mrs. B. watched her daughter walk up to the candle and light it without pride. She noticed the smug looks on some of the other students' faces. She witnessed the honor that some students felt, or even the discomfort at being in the midst of such a formal affair. But as all the inductees stood in a row at the end of the ceremony, there was no contempt in Jeanie's face. No hostility. No smug countenance. Her face wasn't blank, really. She just smiled faintly, and waited. Mrs. B. realized that out of all the kids on the stage she only recognized her daughter. None of Jeanie's friends was there with her; such a simple explanation for all her stubborn noise at the house.

Mrs. B. ran her finger along the top of the frame, dusting it.

Another picture on the wall in the hall was of Jeanie and her grandmother. It was the last picture of the two of them before her grandmother had passed away. They were sitting in the garden under a tree with their backs to the camera. The light filtered through the leaves in such a way that only their faces were lit by the sun. Both of them looked at a single pink rose which had struggled its way through the weeds to stand out in the full sun. The profiles of the women were identical. The old lady's lips were parted in explanation of life, and the young woman listened. It was funny enough to smile, even laugh alone in a hallway, because Jeanie never listened to anyone else but her grandmother. And at the funeral Mrs. B. remembered how Jeanie had insisted on speaking. She had also read a Bible verse, which was written on a tiny piece of paper and remained wedged down in the corner of the picture frame. It read: "Hope deferred makes the heart sick; a wish come true is a staff of life. To despise a word of advice is to ask for trouble; mind what you are told, and you will be rewarded. A wise man's teaching is a fountain of life for one who would escape the snares of death."

Mrs. B. laughed at Jeanie's hypocrisy. She had never taken anyone's advice. Not even her grandmother's after dutifully pretending to listen and learn. What a pity. Jeanie always found a way to prove everyone wrong, or foolish, and probably hadn't thought of the verse since the day her grandmother was buried. But there were the words. Jeanie knew they mattered once. Mrs. B. said, half aloud, "Hope deferred makes the heart sick; like you, my poor child."

She let her eyes pass over Jeanie's high school graduation picture. She glanced at a shot of Jeanie and her father in front of Jeanie's sophomore college dorm that overlooked a lake. Mrs. B. looked for a minute at a picture of all her grown children in front of the Christmas tree. There was another picture just like it from the following year, only Jeanie wasn't there. Mrs. B. reached up and straightened the frame.

She remembered how Jeanie had disappeared two weeks before Christmas. How when she had called her children to breakfast that morning, Jeanie hadn't come down. How they had knocked on her door for over an hour, first annoyed, then anxious, then worried and afraid. Mr. B. and one of their sons had pried the door open with a crowbar, and Mrs. B. half expected to find her daughter dead. It was more of a shock to see the bed neatly made in an empty room. She remembered long searches with the police. She remembered agonizing prayer-filled nights with a God she did not know well enough. She remembered Mr. B. taking them all to the movies to take their minds off things. She remembered finding her youngest son crying in the backyard, and how their oldest daughter did nothing but bake cookies one night. Mrs. B. laughed remembering all the cookies that were made. Every possible kind, six dozen of each. Everyone dealing with the unknown—the excruciating weight of time—in their own way.

Then on Christmas morning, with the bright sun reflecting joy off the snow, there was a phone call. A happy voice filled all the eager receivers in the house with assurance. "Sorry I haven't called. We've been driving forever, and it seems like every gas station's phone is out of order. How stupid is that? Who's we? Oh." She laughed and covered the mouthpiece to scream something at someone nearby. Then back into the phone, "I'm in love. Dad, don't even say it. I know what you'll say, and I say you're wrong. You can fall in love in two weeks, and besides I've known him for almost two months. But the first time we talked was two weeks ago at the bakery. He bought me a jelly doughnut, and I swear it's forever.

"Don't you think it's perfect that I didn't get in touch with you 'til today? No. Well, I think it's perfect. It's like a Christmas present for all of us. So Merry Christmas!" She would have hung up, but someone asked, and she replied, "Oh. Yeah. I'm not really sure. In Arizona somewhere. I'll let you know when I have a real place. Maybe you all can come and visit or something. I can smell the turkey from here, Ma!" But there was no turkey that year. No one had thought of it. They just ate cookies and watched *It's a Wonderful Life*. And they took the picture in front of the tree anyway that year, missing Jeanie.

Mrs. B. took a few more steps toward the living room. She stopped in front of a silly and playful picture of Jeanie and her love. Mrs. B. had never looked at it without smiling, but now she wrinkled her eyebrows and sighed. They must have been camping in the desert. There was a tent and a Coleman stove and a lawn chair. Behind them cacti and sagebrush dotted the landscape all the way to the horizon. There were low mountains on the left side of the picture. It was a joke. Just a snapshot taken by a friend. They had all been drinking. Jeanie was pushing against her love's chest and he, though laughing, had started to fall over. The picture was at least two years old. They had probably wrestled on the ground long after the photographer had forgotten the shot. And Jeanie might only have mailed it for the great smiles on both of their sunlit faces, but in the hall that day, with this boy in her husband's favorite chair, Mrs. B. saw the picture again for the first time. It was devastating to see it so clearly. Her daughter, her mocking, playful, spritely, sarcastic, frivolous, immature, temperamental, evasive, heedless, reckless, unforgiving, so young daughter pushed him away.

Mrs. B. considered turning to the doorway and saying, "Was that verse from Grandma's funeral from Proverbs 13?" But. She didn't ask knowing there'd be no answer.

What must that boy think?

There was a picture that Jeanie had taken of herself. She used a tripod and her father's best camera which had a timer. There was a dark purple thunderhead sky behind her and a rainbow arched itself back over the spruce trees. Jeanie was dressed from head to toe in yellow and stood—arms thrown up—where the rainbow would have touched the ground. A loud statement and strong opinion shouting, "I am a veritable pot of gold, priceless and unattainable." It was a summation. Jeanie with a personality that is impossible to find. Jeanie with a transient confidence that appears comfortable between the harshest, most contrasting conditions, where blazing sun meets the million prisms of an ineffable rain. Jeanie who is only a twist of light. Jeanie, a promise easily broken in a dry Arizona summer.

No one could blame him for his love.

Mrs. B. drew herself up slowly and walked back into the living room. He had gotten up from the chair and was standing in front of the open door near where she had left him. It hadn't been that long. The mat under his feet said, "Welcome Home," and he stared at it.

Neither of them wanted to have to say anything for fear of tears.

But. He was a grown man, not a child, so he said, "Sorry about this, Mrs. B. I thought, well, hell, who knows what I was thinking." He glanced up at her. Her face changed quickly to encourage him with a smile and bright eyes, but he saw her pity first.

She wanted to pull him into some hug that would be enough. But there he was with all the import and fragility of his manhood. *Damn.* She restrained herself, giving whatever support she could by leaving him alone.

He looked down at the shoebox he was holding. There were several small treasures in it. Nothing fancy: a few smooth stones, a picture or two, a blue wax figure of an elephant, a foreign coin, and some other memories no one could possibly share. He laid the box down in the chair he'd gotten up from exhausted from holding such a treasure chest. His hands eased into his pockets and fell asleep at the wrist. He cleared his throat and looked at the clock. He knew that the motion of those hands should mean something, but he didn't see the time. He thought hard. Both of them wished she would just get over it and come out of her room. She didn't. She wouldn't. They both thought she must have fallen asleep by now. They knew her best.

He laughed a little at his own failure and shook his head. With aspiring, raised eyebrows he said, "Well. No sense beating a dead horse, right?" He left before she could see his tears. *Why don't you ever listen?* His car sped away.

Mrs. B. shut the door. Her hand lingered on the doorknob. She looked down at her wedding ring. She moved over to the chair and picked up the box of trinkets. She sat down heavily and picked through them carefully. She lifted out a framed picture of the couple that was wedged in the bottom of the box and made the cardboard sides bow out.

Sighing, she leaned her head back against the chair and held it at arm's length to look at it. They were happy. It was their engagement photo. The one they had taken for the newspaper. The frame was separating at one of the corners. Just a cheap frame from the drug store. Nothing special. Mrs. B. pinched it back together. In a minute she stood up and went to a drawer in the kitchen. She pulled out a hammer and a small nail. She wiped her fingerprints off the glass over the picture with her apron. She walked back to the hallway and found a spot just over the light switch for the picture to hang. She held the tiny frame between her knees and pounded the tiny nail into the wall carefully. She hung the picture and backed away from it. She smiled her own smile as a salute to the two in the picture and turned out the hallway light.

BLUE BUTTERFLY FALLING-OUT BARRETTE

The organ music from a tape recorder on a banged-up, cherry-veneer folding chair in the funeral parlor skips sometimes. People pretend not to notice. They don't want to upset Elise, the young wife of a man who died in a motorcycle accident six days ago. He was too young to die, too old not to know any better, etc. At the wake she stands guard by his casket, for a few last loyal hours.

Honey, we're all so sorry.

Sometimes, Elise, a mourner, or someone else obliged to be in the space to witness the effects of no real cause, looks over at the baby girl, almost a toddler now, but still with a white-ruffled diaper butt. She plays on the floor near a long-stored row of more cherry-wood-veneer folding chairs. Silken hair curls, continually escaping from a blue plastic barrette shaped like a butterfly. She doesn't have enough hair to hold it in place for long. The thing just hangs onto those few fine strands of baby hair that almost always need to be brushed again.

Her mother's pewter pin stay-twists, holds too much wool inside its clasp.

Their eyes meet.

She can stand the shock of sudden death. But not her daughter's big baby eyes. Elise begins to cry, feeling too much *nothing* and too much *all*.

Dressed-up people keep coming. Elise gets it together, holds in her emotions, does her duty. In the middle of another hug, the special pewter pin escapes from its clasp and stabs her near a clavicle. She jumps back from the unintended consequence of the embrace and manages to reclose the pin with blind fingers

below a strained bent-to-see-something-so-close
neck. She does her best. The pin hangs then,
slanted, on a pinched lapel. *That's lovely,* someone
says, not quite to point out the pin's haphazard
arrangement, worse than before.

Elise thinks of stolen future days, begins
to cry, again. The person who hugged her, who
made the pin stab her, leaves, the obligation
having been met. Elise cannot get it together this
time. Tears flow. Friends shuffle, look away,
disperse.

An older man stares at her from a far
corner, then catches himself in the fixation, goes
out the side door to have a cigarette, even though
he shouldn't. He should want to quit.

Inside still the white-ruffled diaper butt,
patent leather shoes, and blue butterfly falling-out
barrette come crawling out with their toddler curls
from under a wooden folding chair missing some
veneer. A nearby ancient matron's voice says,
Why. There you are!

Not wanting to understand quite so very
much from that tone of voice the white-ruffled

diaper butt moves back under the row of wooden folding chairs. Back away from the *Why. There you are!* ancient lady, who—after a despairing minute after accosting such a shy child—falls asleep, doesn't notice three little fingers working their slow, curious way into the brass-hinged pinch point.

Elise stops shuddering convulsively when her mother takes her elbow and whispers. The sequence repeats. The pewter pin on Elise's lapel pops open again. Instead of allowing it to stab her this time, having adapted, Elise hears the little rotating clasp click over, feels the pin loosen, steps back from the three-hundredth hug. She lets the pin fall, lost.

Instinctively Elise's eyes travel to the floor, demanding to find the pewter gift with all its significance among the weeds in the ornate carpet garden. Unnecessarily, several men—old and young, all hovering, useless—leap to action: leaning over, each hoping to be the one to pick up the precious pin, to offer it back, to be helpful, to do something other than flirt with the floor.

Still snoozing, the *Why. There you are!* ancient lady amply shifts in her seat.

Three fingers, baby girl almost-a-toddler-now fingers, twist and pop. Soft bloody broken bones get crushed somewhere inside the chair.

Why. There you are! dozing wakes startled, reacts haphazardly to the wailing scream of the child underneath her in agony and so changes instantly to, *Oh my dear Lord in Heaven. I didn't know you were down there, Sweet Pea. Dear Heavens. Oh no. Oh God. Don't cry, precious girl. I didn't mean to. I am so sorry.*

Hugging no one in that moment, unwilling really, Elise moves away from her post near the casket, walks over to her child in another slow-motion refusal to panic, picks the little girl up ruffled behind and all, and lets her bleed onto the best white silk blouse she's ever owned for two days.

Red face screams over a shoulder as the pace picks up and the young mother hurries down the aisle of chairs, through the door, across the patchy August grass to her car, and all the way to the county's emergency room.

What can anyone do?

At the funeral home people disperse as quickly as is appropriate, which is unclear. The old woman who was in the chair is a wreck. She gets comforted by Elise's mother, who hates her, always has. Even they go, individually, after a while.

The flowers stay.

The last person, an older man, not a great-uncle, but someone who would have probably stopped over to the house anyway, picks up the blue butterfly barrette. He thumbs it open, feels its tiny open-hinged plastic bed of nails, clasps the thing tight again, and drops it, already forgotten, into his pocket.

DEAD RECKONING WITH AZIMUTH

I don't suppose you would ever believe
that this entire book happens in just two minutes.
But it does. It's overwhelmed and hyperbolic,
complete with clenched chest, sweats, and hives.
It happens right there. Where? Right there in the
two minutes that you absolutely must sit down in
the shaded sands of Chicago's North Avenue
beach. Don't collapse. That's ridiculous. And. No.
Don't go over on the bench. Definitely not that
bench. Why do you think no one's on it? There's
something sticky there. Stop! What are you
thinking? Where are you going? No. My God. Of

course not by the water. That's almost fifty yards from here. It's much too far to cross the beach when this disoriented. Just sit down. Wherever you are, just sit right down. Yes, yes, yes. Come on. At least try to be aware of where you are physically. And. So. Fine. Great. Excellent. Good. There you go. Here you are. South of Fullerton. North of the quaint brick bathrooms. You know. Quit worrying. Look around. Look at anything. Look here. Look. Look. Look at whatever will help you just calm the fuck down. Come on. Relax. I already said this whole thing happens in just two minutes. So. For a book that short, what more do you need for a setting? Time and place. That's it. That's the requirement. You're golden. You know. That's what you want. That's what you need. To know. Right? To stop your mind from racing. Yes? So. Okay. Good. You know. You're not on the pavement of the lakeshore path. You're not down by the water or in anybody's way. You're not on the bench with that two-day-old sticky Popsicle residue. It's not summer but it's an abnormally hot day in spring or fall. Maybe even one of those completely freakish December days when it hits eighty degrees in the Midwest. There's a bit of shade, perhaps, yes, hopefully, yes, okay, good, fine, great, sure, yes, there's an opportunity to collect yourself, maybe call a friend, maybe take a few breaths, maybe the eyes keep roving, keep gleaning, keep noticing something pleasant to look at: if it's not December then a volleyball game, a lifeguard walking back and forth with one of those bright orangey-red rocket-shaped flotation devices with the harpoon cording, or, you know, whatever: the sky, the seven, the seventy-two, the one hundred forty-nine gulls all, each, there together preening on the breakwater, the pebbles in the sand, the bikers weaving past each other in the bike path flux, the joggers—all fists and elbows—the Mexican families grilling on the lawn, the black guy people-watching from the bench further down, the white guy trudging along getting back in shape after what could have been a second heart attack, the Asian woman training for another triathlon, and the chatty happy parents with strollers. It's all there.

ACKNOWLEDGMENTS

This book arose out of the four books of the *On Impulse* series. It seems a bit redundant to list everyone who helped with all those other books. So. For this quiet labor of love it's probably enough to thank Morgan, Elliott, Max, MJ, Skip, Oh Andy, David, Adam, Mom, Noel, Jim, Dave, Steph, Timothy, Truda, Nate, Tammy, Ryan, Adam, my Wednesday night family, Italian openness on Fridays, candles on Sundays, Gus, Alan, JT, Eric, Aunt Lucy, Darren Mast, Mark Rayburn, Jeff Rayburn, Bill Boehler, Martha, Scott, Joy, Grant, Julianna, Joseph, Andy, Hannah, Gin Y. Havard, and David McNamara.

ABOUT THE AUTHOR

Best New American Voices nominee Nath Jones received an MFA in creative writing from Northwestern University. Her publishing credits include PANK *Magazine*, *There Are No Rules*, and *Sailing World*. She lives and writes in Chicago.

ABOUT THE EDITOR

Morgan Kiger is a chronic consumer of printed goods, an activist for animal welfare, a cooker and eater of seasonal deliciousness, and first-time editor. She resides in San Francisco, CA with her husband, Elliott, and the most popular dog in the city, Baron Maxwell Maverick von Scrufferson.

ABOUT THE ON IMPULSE SERIES

*

We all have an impulse to share our experience. The first four collections of short works explore storytelling from catharsis to craft. The writing style develops from the raw, associative, tyrannic rambles of cathartic non-fiction, flash fiction, and rant in *The War is Language ala* our digital domains, to the rough-hewn vignettes of *2000 Deciduous Trees*, into the compact characterizations of the tellings in *Love & Darts*, and finally toward *Acquainted with Squalor*'s fully-crafted short stories that use literary devices to reveal a world well-rendered.